TIGER'S GAMBIT

SHIFTERS' MATES BOOK 1

MINETTE MOREAU

Cover art by Wicked Smart Designs
Editing provided by Amy Briggs

E-book ISBN: 978-1-952596-24-7
Print ISBN: 978-1-952596-25-4

PROLOGUE

RENATA

S endra closed her book and peered down at me, her brown eyes sharp. She adjusted the fussy lace collar buttoned to her chin and brushed a stray hair from her blue dress. "Did you enjoy the story?"

"Yes, but I still prefer Shakespeare."

Chuckling, she patted my head. Her patronizing touch made me feel like a cub, as did my uncomfortable position on the floor at her feet.

"It's important to explore literature, Miss Andreyev. You might find something else you enjoy just as much." Her smile faded as she took the book and put it on the table next to her chair. "We have to talk."

I stood and stretched, my back cracking. "What about?"

"I want you to go to the Exodus Authority."

"I don't need or want a mate." I returned her teacup to the kitchen. It hadn't held tea, of course. It was just filtered and boiled water, but she liked the tiny reminder of life before the storms that had been slowly destroying all life on Earth.

"Have you considered cubs?"

"Why bother?" I left the cup in the sink and went to her bookshelf. "Do you want me to read? I can almost do *Gulliver's Travels*."

I refused to talk about cubs. They weren't an option for either of us. Sendra was too old, and I'd never found a male worth a mating bite. Although the few Ximerans I'd seen hadn't been cruel or unappealing, I had no idea if any of them would make a good mate. Living on Earth wasn't easy, but I had no idea what Ximera was like. The Ximerans promised a bountiful, sustainable environment with the resources to feed the population, but what if they lied? If things didn't work out with my mate, would they let me stay? I couldn't come back to Earth.

Pussy. There will be prey there.

I ignored my tiger's caustic comment as Sendra sighed and shook her head. "I'm going to ground. I want you to give a sample and—"

"No." The book I'd chosen tumbled to the floor, my fingers unable to hold its weight. "I keep you safe here."

"I'm afraid not even the mighty tiger can protect someone from old age. My jackal and I have seen too much, and she's very tired."

"I said no." I picked up the book and slammed it into place, making the bookcase shudder. "It's a stupid idea. I won't let you do that."

"You can't stop death." She was silent for a moment, then added, "It comes for everyone, sooner or later."

I shivered at her hollow whisper. "Try me."

She growled, the low rumble vibrating her thin frame. Without warning, she sprang at me and opened a gash on my face with her claws, leaving me bleeding. I covered the wound with my hand and stared at her in shock.

"Why are you doing this?"

"You are no longer welcome here, Miss Andreyev, and you're too stubborn to do as you're told. Leave now and do as I've asked." Blood dripped from her claws as she crouched and leapt for me again.

I dodged out of the way, upsetting her table and chair. She hissed, her teeth bared.

Tears welled in my eyes, and I backed away from her, shaking my head in denial. "I can't leave like this."

Fangs glistened between her thin lips. "I'm over a hundred years old, cub. I'm going to die, and I prefer to do it on my own. You're going to leave this place and find a mate and have cubs. That is all I want from you."

"But—"

She snarled, and I ducked when she threw a book at my head. I held out both hands as I backed away. "Okay. I just..." I sniffed against the tears thickening behind my eyes. "I'll miss you, Sendra."

She didn't answer, and I left her den, my tears falling to mix with the blood on my face. I'd abandoned my best friend, and I couldn't imagine my life without her. Without Sendra, there was nothing for me on Earth.

I sobbed, the breath tearing in my throat as I ran. A human darted across the street to avoid me, engaging my tiger's prey drive, but he was too old and sick to provide any sport. I left him alone and kept running, not knowing or caring where I was going.

The cut on my cheek itched as it closed, but I didn't bother to wipe the blood away. I wondered if Sendra had attacked me in the hope I'd ease her passing. One swipe of a claw across her throat would have done it. I just couldn't. She would sneer and call me weak and too emotional, but she'd been my only friend for my entire adult life.

Everyone knew the story of Earth's fall from grace. Seven years of solar storms knocked out our ecosystem almost a hundred years ago. Humans might have handled the resulting ice age, but the collapse of humanity was ultimately caused by such a simple thing. Bees. The honeybee that pollinated most food crops became extinct before the third year. It was humanity's swan song.

Sendra told me tigers had been considered royalty back then and jackals weren't considered at all. Before the storms, we wouldn't have been friends. I'd never felt like royalty though. The throne of the Andreyev tigers had long been crushed under the weight of poisoned destruction.

I tugged my jacket closer against the frigid breeze. Atlanta used to have hot summer weather, but the few people left in the city were lucky if daytime temperatures reached fifty in August. October would bring several feet of snow. The reek of poison and dying things filled the air and never cleared, even after the spring rains.

I slowed when I reached the carcass of my tree; one of the few bits of organic material left in old Atlanta. I always came to visit her when I was upset about something. I had no idea why I'd always thought of the tree as female. My bench was still there, a piece of stained marble with a chunk of concrete under one broken leg next to a statue of a man in a long robe. He had such a peaceful expression on his face, even though half his head was cracked away. The ruins of an old hospital surrounded the tree, its doors and windows long since scavenged, leaving gaping holes in the red brick.

I sat down and patted her lifeless trunk, leaning back to stare into skeletal branches. I tried to imagine what she must have looked like. I wanted to picture her with leaves, but I'd never seen a living plant except in Sendra's books.

My tree would stand forever, dead, but a lasting testament to life on Earth. The empty hulks of concrete that had housed businesses and homes were the humans' mark on the planet, but she was true evidence of life that existed beyond the machinations of humans. I closed my eyes, soaking in the peace of this sacred place and tried to remember how to pray.

"Pretty girl. We'll have some fun and take that nice jacket she's wearing."

I heaved out a sigh and rolled my eyes. Although I couldn't see the four men behind the south wall of the abandoned hospital, the fools thought they were far enough away I wouldn't hear them. I patted my tree one last time and left the dead garden, unwilling to foul my private space with a fight.

I had too much on my mind to make much sport of them, so I led them toward a quiet alley away from the clusters of occupied houses. They were either idiots or were new in town. Everyone in this neighborhood knew the only predator allowed in the city was me.

Their evil laughter followed me, and I quickened my pace, wanting only to get the task over with and take care of the one thing Sendra had asked of me. The alley widened into a small courtyard, ending at a rusted chain-link fence blocked by abandoned cars on the other side. There was enough room to get behind them and cut off their escape. I smelled their excitement as they hurried toward me.

"Wait up, pretty!" The largest of the four shouted after me as I reached the fence. He was the only one who didn't look on the brink of starvation, and it marked him as our first kill.

They spread out, thinking they had me trapped. The men wore heavy packs on their backs with bedrolls tied to them. Though I didn't see a gun, I smelled the acrid scent of oil and metal. Knitted hoods covered their faces. My nose twitched at the stench of violence and hate emanating from them.

"Hey, little girl! Give us that jacket and maybe we won't hurt you too badly! I'll even give you a cut on the other side of your face so you're sym... Sym... something." He grinned, showing blackened teeth as he pulled a worn knife from his pocket. The stupid thing wasn't even four inches long. My claws were longer. Emboldened by the fence at my back, he moved closer, brandishing his poor weapon.

"I believe symmetrical is the word you're too stupid to find."

His face wrinkled into a vicious grimace of hate. "I'm gonna cut you good for that, bitch!"

I held my tiger back as I waited for them to get closer. We would end this threat to our home and distribute their belongings to the needy. There was an elderly couple a few blocks from our den who could use their warm clothes and whatever they carried.

The large one rushed me with his knife held high, and allowed my tiger her freedom. We heard the humans' curses as mist covered us. In the scant second during our shift, I could stare into her fathomless blue eyes, as she could into mine. It was the single moment we had no physical shape and knew each other as separate beings sharing a single body. Then fur popped and flowed over my body; the sensation like ants on my skin. Bones ground against joints as they changed shape and moved, and the sharp pain was gone within seconds. The leader dropped his knife and took a single step backward. We wrinkled our muzzle into a snarl as we waited, enjoying the moment of shocked silence before the screams.

When our task was done, I pushed the tiger aside and returned to my human form, pulling on the clothes I'd left in a heap when I shifted. I didn't bother rummaging through their packs as I stripped the bodies and rolled their clothes into a blanket I'd retrieved from one of the bedrolls. They had nothing I wanted, but my elderly neighbors might find something of value once the items were cleaned.

An old woman stood at the alley entrance, her threadbare coat pulled close around her frail body, the hood concealing her hair. I didn't know her but recognized her scent. She nodded once and turned to walk away.

"Wait!" I caught up to her and handed her the warm coat the gang leader had been wearing. My neighbors didn't need so much. Tears filled her eyes, and she gave me a hard hug before hurrying away. I shivered at the sensation of being touched by a stranger as I continued toward my destination. It wasn't unpleasant, but it was... odd. Humans never touched me willingly.

Earth wasn't much of a tourist destination these days, but men from a system called Ximera had been collecting human women for almost two years, using genetic tests to match potential mates.

I wasn't interested in a mate. They left you alone when they died.

Just like my father had done to my mother. Sendra had been right though. I couldn't survive here forever. Although humans managed to grow some food, hoarding heirloom seeds that were worth more than gold had once been, there was no prey, and no chance for a cub.

Would it be so bad to leave a dying planet? Sendra had been after me for months to go, but I'd refused to admit to myself that sheer age would take her long before I was ready to let her go. Without Sendra, there wasn't anything stopping me.

"All right, you skinny old bitch. I'm going!" It had to have been my imagination, but I thought I heard her rusty laugh behind me as I made my way to the Exodus Authority.

I crossed the broken pavement leading to the stadium's main entrance. A human guard let me through the makeshift barricade, and I stood in line behind several other women. I wondered how many would find mates in this Faustian bargain.

When it was my turn, a human nurse drew a blood sample and took my picture, then told me to come back in two days for my results. I wasn't sure what I wanted the answer to be, nor did I have any idea what they expected to find. Maybe they were looking for genetic disease or other infirmity. Considering my reading skills were a little iffy—at least according to Kendra—and I didn't know the first thing about medicine or healing, it was likely I wouldn't have understood if they'd tried to explain it.

CHAPTER
ONE

RAKON

"Does this thing never shut up?" I couldn't disguise my irritation, and I slapped the comm to silence it. "Increase speed by three percent."

My co-pilot muttered, but he was too obedient to question my orders. I should have been paying attention to the panel in front of me. Lights flashed and sirens blared as we approached the wormhole leading toward the dying planet that hosted my female, yet I couldn't. Her image was all I saw.

The picture submitted with the genetic match revealed a tall, angular woman with wide hips. The rest of her body was concealed by a black jacket. Her hair was gold with dark streaks, and she had blue eyes. She clutched her jacket closed in the photo, but she was too thin, and I knew she hadn't been eating properly. I frowned at the image and tapped the screen to enlarge it, realizing someone had struck her. My blood boiled at the healing cut on her cheek, and I hoped I would have enough time to track down whoever had marred her pretty face.

It was going to be fourteen Earth days before I could get to her, and it was unconscionable that a branded Ximeran Warlord should have to wait for anything he desired. But wait I must, because the laws of propulsion and gravity would not bow to my will.

More's the pity.

"Commander Rakon, communication from High Council on your comm link."

I would give my battle commission to silence that damned Council, but I managed to smooth my scowl into a less threatening expression. When the screen loaded, I said, "What can I do for you today, Councilor?"

Councilor Harkon's pudgy face filled the screen. His thick lips curled into a derisive smirk under muddy brown eyes, and the dome of his bald head gleamed.

"We hear you're on your way to collect your specimen."

Renata Andreyev was not a specimen, but I managed to dredge up a bland smile that hid my annoyance. "Yes, Councilor. It has been determined that she is my genetic mate."

"Turn your ship around. The human Andreyev has been loaded into a transport and is en route. You are needed elsewhere."

"I see. May I have the identification of this transport?"

"I don't know it, and it doesn't matter. Your specimen will arrive in approximately two Earth weeks as you intended. We require your presence in the seventeenth sector. The mission details should be loaded into your computer already."

"Yes, Councilor Harkon." I cut off the comm, ignoring his last few words.

Although every inch of my body wanted to keep going toward my mate, I did as I was ordered and turned my cruiser around toward sector seventeen. That sector was a perpetual thorn in my side, filled with bounty hunters, slavers, and the dregs of interstellar society. If they behaved themselves, we left them alone. No one could say they didn't serve a purpose. Nearly everyone took advantage of delicacies only available from the smugglers. Wine and spirits, rare foods, and textiles all found their way through sector seventeen for distribution elsewhere.

I didn't understand why the Council was intruding on my task, but it didn't matter. I didn't give a fuck about the black market, or about whoever I would have to kill in sector seventeen. In two weeks, pretty Renata with the white-gold-and-black hair would be in my bed.

Would she like me? I wished my mother was still alive to help me with her, but she'd died of the same wasting disease that took most of our females. Damned Krenions. I wish there was one left so I could kill it, but I'd already destroyed the last of the pestilential species who had introduced the devastating plague a dozen cycles ago. And good riddance.

Pushing the thoughts away, I checked our location. I'd reach sector seventeen in a few days. That would give me plenty of time to scan my collection of old Earth vids. I loved *Golden Girls*. Earth females were almost indistinguishable from their Ximeran counterparts, and Blanche reminded me of my mother. Maybe I liked it because I hadn't seen an aged female in... I couldn't remember the last time.

The vids became popular when it was discovered humans could be potential mates. We shared a similar physical appearance, though Ximerans tended to be larger. Humans also had a wide variety of skin and hair coloration, ranging from shimmery black to skin as pale as the blossoms of an *orcan* tree. Ximerans weren't lucky enough to enjoy such diversity. Our scientists told us we shared a common ancestor with humans, although it had been many hundreds of thousands of cycles ago.

Most Ximerans watched those old vids to get some idea of Earth culture, along with assistance in learning English. Though humans had a vast number of languages, we'd chosen the one used most for telecommunications and transport. Their lives seemed strange, but the vids were a hundred Earth years old. The Ximeran cycle was close enough to a year to make the difference negligible.

Things were different now. I'd seen what was left of Earth. The storms had destroyed nearly everything, and I was shocked anything had survived. Humans must have been a very resourceful species.

Nothing I watched helped me find something to woo the beauty on her way to me. The vids were ancient and from a time when the planet had been healthy. I turned my attention to the planet's literature. Unlike the vids, the books had short synopses, allowing me to search by keyword. Mates and joining produced nothing of note, so I tried love and marriage, terms I'd heard before in the humans' lexicon.

That search produced more titles than I cared to manage, but one caught my eye because it was just a few hundred pages. It had a picture of a couple locked in an embrace, with the male's arms wrapped tightly around his female as she gazed up at him.

When I finished, I closed out the book and chose another of the same type. If the first was to be believed, a male need only be rich and give a female pleasure until she fell gratefully into his arms. I met the first requirement and was determined to meet the second.

From the two books, I learned the mistakes the males made that hurt or angered their females. Blackmail, confinement, harsh words, and humiliation. Those human males were a cocky bunch and lucky their mates were gentle creatures. None of that would have gone over with Ximeran females. A male would have come back missing body parts—if he lived to come back at all.

~

RENATA

I was at the Exodus Authority an hour past dawn on the third day after I'd given my sample. I'd spent the last two days watching Sendra's den in the misguided hope that she would come to her senses and forget her wish to die.

No one answered my knock. No one twitched a curtain or lit any lamps. There was no scent or sound of movement. I cried as I walked away, knowing she was already gone. My tiger yowled in a vain attempt to get me to pay attention. In this world, emotion got you dead. I couldn't afford to show my grief in public.

I hid in the remains of a building to give myself time to calm down. I sat there for hours, watching women walk in and out. I wanted to laugh at their hopeful expressions. One cried as she walked straight into the arms of a human man just a few feet away from my hiding spot.

If I didn't have my tiger's hearing, I'd have missed her soft whisper. "I didn't give them my blood, Seth."

"Lisa, you promised." The man took her hand and pressed his lips to her gloved palm. "You promised you'd go if they found a match."

She stopped walking and looked up into his face. She put her hands on his cheeks and tears streamed from her eyes. "I know. I just... I couldn't. A life without you is no life at all. Whatever time we have left, I want to spend it with you."

"Oh, honey."

I smelled the man's tears as he took his woman into his arms. My chest ached at what he'd been willing to sacrifice for her, and a sob choked me as it tried to escape my throat. I couldn't fathom a love so deep. I watched them for a long time as they walked away.

When I couldn't see them anymore, I shouldered my pack and walked toward the stadium. I didn't know if I would find that kind of love on Ximera, but I knew I wouldn't find it on Earth.

The human guard stepped in front of the barricade as I approached. "State your name and business, please."

"Renata Andreyev. I'm here to find out the results of my blood test."

The guard's eyes brightened. "We've been waiting for you. Follow me, please." He led me down a hall into a small room furnished with a metal table and two chairs.

"Have a seat. The Magistrate will be with you shortly."

The door shut behind the guard with a metallic clang. I flinched at the noise. My tiger paced in my head, uncomfortable with the confinement.

Several minutes later, the door opened, revealing a human male followed by a tall figure. I thought it was male, but I wasn't sure. Even my tiger was confused, and we loathed the creature on sight. It reeked of old blood and violence. My tiger wanted to kill it, and I couldn't disagree. I soothed her with a single word.

"Soon," I whispered. The single word calmed her, but she didn't stand down.

The creature either didn't notice my reaction, or it didn't care. I forced myself to listen to the human's words.

"I am Magistrate Smith. I'm responsible for administering the exchange program between Earth and Ximera. Blood tests have determined that you are the genetic mate of Warlord Rakon of Ximera 8."

He placed a tablet on the table, bearing a single image of the male my blood told them would be my future mate. My tiger sniffed in derision, but I ignored her. Instead of an unknown alien male, I had a name and a face. And I liked what I saw.

Rakon was bulky with muscle under a skintight black uniform. Weapons were sheathed at his narrow hips, making him look dangerously competent. Unflinchingly, his dark brown eyes met the camera, stern, yet filled with excitement. Black hair fell past his shoulders in an inky trail, and my fingers itched to touch the dark strands.

I'd never seen a more visually appealing male. He stood next to a doorway with marks denoting his height. His head reached well past the two-meter mark. Thick eyebrows curved upwards at the ends, trailing into a point high on his temples. A stylized brand marked the skin under his left eye, swirling into an infinity symbol on his jaw. He obviously wasn't human; he was too damned big for that. Aside from his size, his bone structure was almost catlike, with high cheekbones, square jaw, and tilted eyes. His nose was thin and aquiline, with a small bump in the middle as if it had been broken and poorly set.

"I accept."

The tiger yowled at me, displeasure evident in every note. I didn't care. I liked the look of this Rakon and couldn't understand why she didn't. He was gloriously male, and the most beautiful being I'd ever seen. I wanted to see him. Smell him. We had to wait until we could catch his scent before we refused him. "Will there be grass and fresh air?"

"Of course. Ximera 8 has a clean and healthy environment." The human gave me a wide smile and pulled me into a brief hug. I flinched at the touch, reminding my tiger that the Magistrate meant no harm, yet I didn't understand why strangers were so determined to hug me now when it had never happened before. "I wish you the best of luck, Miss Andreyev. When you're ready to leave, Mr. Morris will escort you to your shuttle."

"Thank you." I shook his hand and turned to face the pale creature. It gave me a sneering smile and claws erupted from my fingertips. I balled my fists to hide them but wanted nothing more than to remove its face from the front of its head. I soothed the tiger with images of taking half its skull for good measure.

Aggravated chuffing told me she wasn't appeased. I told her we could kill Rakon and his transport crew if he wasn't pleasing.

They allowed me an hour to pack, but I didn't need it. I carried everything I cared about. The creature escorted me through the empty space in the center of the stadium and up a ramp into a waiting ship. I flinched when the ramp slid into the hull and the bulkhead doors slammed, cutting off any chance of escape. A cold hand touched my arm, and I jerked away. How could its hand be so icy through the thick leather of my jacket?

"Don't touch," I hissed.

The creature's face rearranged itself into what I thought was a frown, but it nodded. "Fine, human. Follow me."

It led me past several others of the same species. They were all pale, almost stick-thin, and all bore the stench of old blood. My nose wrinkled, and I had to stop myself from opening my mouth in the feral grimace Sendra had called a Flehmen Response. It was a weird name for a way to better taste scents. I didn't want to taste this odor though. My tiger and I both knew what that sweet, coppery stench was.

We reached an open doorway revealing a miniscule chamber I assumed would be my quarters for the trip. There was a tiny bed that might not be long enough for me, a small metal table, one chair, and a vid screen. It was claustrophobic, but I wouldn't have to be here for long. In two weeks, I would meet my potential mate.

I walked inside and turned around to thank the creature, but to my surprise and increasing trepidation, he chuckled. The sound burbled wetly in his throat, sickening me as he pressed a button on the wall. The door slid closed with a solid whump, and I tried to quell my rising panic. Maybe they didn't want me wandering around while the ship escaped Earth's atmosphere. Maybe they wanted to keep me safe. Maybe...

None of my thoughts helped. I hated being trapped. No cat likes a cage, and I was worse than most. I supposed I could shift, but the room was too small to contain me if I went furry. The chamber was barely two meters square and didn't even have enough space for pacing. I sat down on the cot, grimacing at the hard surface. I hadn't thought I'd be traveling in luxury, but this was ridiculous.

I inhaled a calming breath, only then noticing the air had a sweet tinge I'd never encountered. The scent was almost sickening and soon became overwhelming. I opened my mouth, but the odor crossing my sensitive palate made me gag and spit. When my eyes grew heavy, I realized the odor was a drug.

Why would the creatures want me unconscious? It didn't make any sense. I tried to shift, damning the small space, but the tiger refused to come forth. Black stripes formed on my hands, but I couldn't finish and collapsed to the hard floor.

I heard laughter as the cadaverous alien returned and tossed me over its shoulder. It carried me down a corridor, its heavy footfalls echoing against metal. When we stopped moving forward, the alien pushed me off its shoulder onto a hard surface. I tried to open my eyes, but nothing worked. It might have been for the best though. Wherever I'd been taken was so brightly illuminated that it hurt my eyes through the closed lids.

It rolled me to my back and straightened my limbs, chattering in a guttural language I didn't understand. I heard a slam as something dropped over my head, but I didn't have enough muscle control to flinch. Even though I couldn't see, I knew I'd been closed into something. Was it a cage or a stasis unit? I'd never seen one, but I knew of their existence.

A stasis unit meant one of two things. The aliens wanted me safely out of the way and contained for the trip, or I was going farther than was convenient without one. I hoped it wasn't the latter.

Fresh air blew across my face, and I sucked in a lungful of the untainted breeze as the temperature dropped rapidly. The air changed and became thick with the drug the alien had used on me earlier. Holding my breath for just a moment, I had enough presence of mind to thank whatever deity people prayed to that they hadn't shackled me.

Someone was going to be very sorry when I came out of stasis.

CHAPTER

TWO

RAKON

Harkon smirked at me from behind his desk, his soft hands folded in front of him. "I'm afraid we can't grant your leave, Commander. You're needed in—"

"Don't bother."

His face turned purple, and he slammed his fist down on his desk when I turned to leave. "I have not dismissed you!"

There was something very wrong here. I knew Harkon hated me. The feeling was mutual. It didn't explain why Renata wasn't in my house waiting for me. She'd never landed on Ximera 8. Port Commander Denkar could find no record of her taking passage on any Ximeran ship.

Administrators and staff scattered in the wake of my heavy footsteps as I pounded down the corridor to First Councilor Fengar's office.

To his credit, Fengar's assistant took one look at my face and gestured toward the inner sanctum. "He's inside, sir."

"Thanks." I knocked, opening the door without waiting for an answer.

The First set aside a tablet and gestured toward a chair in front of his massive desk. "Where's the fire, boy?"

"I need to request a leave of absence, sir."

"For what purpose?" His lips pursed, and he added, "And for how long?"

"My mate is missing. She left Earth approximately fifteen Earth days ago, but there is no record of her transport. I want to find out where she went."

His eyes widened and he swore, then scrawled his signature across a blank leave certification. "What are you waiting for?" he asked, thrusting it at me. "Get out of here."

Fourteen days later, I stood in the ruins of a gaming complex, arguing with an elderly human male.

"What do you mean she's gone?" I lifted the frightened and angry human off his feet. I could have used comm links for communication with Magistrate Smith, but I wanted to look into his eyes while he explained how he'd lost my mate. And if someone had stolen her, I'd be that much closer to the trail.

The human pointed a shaking finger at a desk scattered with paper. "She boarded a transport a month ago. My assistant, Jensen, arranged the delivery. The order is on the desk."

I dropped him and pointed at the mass of paper littering the surface. "Find it."

He rifled through the detritus and eventually found what I wanted. "Here. It's dated and signed."

I snatched the paper away and scanned it. Renata had indeed been loaded on an unnamed transport. I entered the call number into my comm and found that it was registered to a holding company located in... Sector seventeen, of course.

Why I hadn't blown that entire sector into bits when I'd had the chance was beyond me.

"Describe the appearance of the being who took her." I understood it was customary to say please, but I was too impatient.

"Unpleasant," the human said. "Pale and thin, about nine feet tall, with protruding eyes. Didn't smell like he bathed much. He had an order of transport from the Ximeran Council. It's with the rest of her documentation."

The humans had a word. *Fuck.* That single word encompassed the physical act of copulation, disgust, anger, and astonishment. I'd learned it from Earth television. The human cowered when I used it.

Apparently, we hadn't been as thorough at eradicating the Krenions as we'd thought. I tried to remind myself that it wasn't the human's fault. Nobody had considered mentioning that any Krenion was to be shot on sight. They were supposed to be extinct in all systems surrounding Ximera.

I gritted my teeth, praying to the old gods for patience. "If you see one of those creatures again, you shoot first. Blow them out of the sky if you can."

The human's eyes widened in surprise. "What? Why would we do that?"

"They're responsible for killing all the females in the Ximeran system. If we find humans have knowingly harbored any Krenion, we will not hesitate to eradicate this planet." I gripped the fabric at the human's throat and lifted him off the floor. "Do you understand?"

The human's face filled with sick anger and resolution. "I wish you had told us," he gritted out past the chokehold I had on his neck. "What can we do to help you find her?"

"Is Renata the only human you've sent with them?"

"No. There are four more."

He wriggled free, and I let him go to rummage through more paper. "Ah, here." He handed me a thick file. "Here are the dossiers on the other women, including their pictures and genetic results. Soledad Martinez and her sisters, Ursula and Tereza, were taken approximately twelve months ago, and Chen Daiyu left a few weeks before Renata."

The human wrung his hands. "Why didn't you tell us? I'm worried sick about them. What if the Krenions..." He let the question hang.

"We thought they were extinct. I was on the mission to cleanse their lair. I personally ripped the throat out of the last one."

"Apparently not." The human frowned angrily. "Look. These women are human, citizens of whatever is left of Earth. I know we don't have any power. We can barely keep ourselves alive. But I swear to God, if you don't fix this..."

My anger faded. This old human, so fierce, so angry at what he saw as a Ximeran failure, threatened me, knowing he was weak, knowing he had no way to make the threat stick. The only thing he could do would be to prevent our access to human females.

That wasn't acceptable. Hundreds of Ximeran males had already found mates here without issue. The females had been transported on private carriers in comfort and luxury, meeting their new mates on arrival. I had to question what it was about these particular females that drew Krenion attention.

"The Krenions only came for the Martinez sisters, Chen, and Renata, correct?"

"Yes, but Daiyu is Chinese."

"What?"

"Chen is her family name. The Chinese have family names first."

"What's so special about these women?" I paced the length of the small office, the file clutched in my hand.

"They all have an extra chromosome. They're dormant as far as we can tell, and the ladies were otherwise healthy, but all five have forty-seven instead of forty-six."

That didn't make any sense. Even in a species as alien as humans, chromosomes would come in pairs. "You say forty-six is the usual number for humans? Perhaps there was an error with the blood test."

"That's the weird thing." The human sighed and rubbed his face. "It's an unpaired chromosome, and we ran the test twice on all five women. We don't know what it means. Most of our medical knowledge is gone, but I seem to remember that an unpaired chromosome is either inconsistent with life or will manifest in visible ways. The women were thin, but healthier than all the others we've sent to Ximera."

I spread the file on the desk. All the females were astonishingly beautiful, though too thin as the human had mentioned. I pulled up a picture of Renata from my tablet. Her eyes were blue, while the other four females had dark brown eyes. Yet when I looked closer at their pupils, I realized they weren't round. It wasn't enough to note a difference on a cursory exam, but they weren't the same shape as those of the human male in front of me.

I scanned the file. Daiyu had been matched with Warlord Dakar. Dakar would be a good mate for the silver-haired beauty, and was known to be a considerate lover, if somewhat remote. I turned the sheet over to learn about Soledad's intended.

"Oh, fuck me." Soledad's sisters had been matched with males I didn't know, but I wasn't sure I cared. This was going to be bad.

"What? What's wrong?"

I hadn't realized I'd said the words out loud, but I ignored the human, holding up a hand demanding silence. Soledad was a dark thing, dark hair, black eyes, dusky skin. Spots dusted the skin on her face, random blotches of pigmentation that looked like camouflage. And her eyes were terrifying. Feral and black and utterly emotionless.

Renata's eyes were strange, both for the sparkling blue color and for the elongated pupil, but there was emotion in them. Fear and determination, but emotion. Soledad was... scary. Maybe it would help her, but I doubted it. She'd been matched with Warlord Markon.

I knew Markon. We'd grown up together. I'd watched him hold his mate as she died from the Krenion's virus. I'd helped to restrain him when he'd tried to follow her into death. He'd never forgiven me for it.

"I have to go." I held out my hand. It was a strange gesture, but humans seemed to expect the courtesy of a handshake. The human took my hand and pumped it up and down a few times before letting it go.

"Will you find them?"

"Yes." There was no question in my mind. I would find the last few Krenions and end them like I'd done to the rest of their kind. The Council would probably throw a fit over my next order, but they could suck my cock over it. "No human female leaves this planet unless her matched mate comes to collect her."

The human chuckled. "I'd already planned on giving that order. If you want those girls bad enough, come fetch them yourselves." He stared at me, intelligence and residual anger flickering in his eyes. "You Ximerans made me risk my people, knowing we have no way of protecting them. It won't happen again."

My mouth gaped open and I snapped it shut. "Good."

I wouldn't even be blamed for the order. It had been a human decision. I held in my chuckle, knowing it wouldn't be taken well.

It would be a long trip back to sector seventeen, but I needed the time to think. I needed to know what was special about the females the Krenions had stolen, aside from their odd genetics. I needed to contact Markon and Dakar so they could search for their mates. Dakar likely already knew about Daiyu, but Markon was often out of communication range as he patrolled the outer sectors looking for a particularly nasty pirate pillaging the outposts. He would never have voluntarily submitted a sample for testing. Someone, perhaps one of the medical staff during his yearly checkups, had probably stolen some bit of genetic material. I didn't know how he would take the news, or who he would kill when he found out.

~

RENATA

Cool air blew across my skin, and I winced against the bright lights in my eyes. I didn't get a chance to wonder how long I'd been out, or who had removed my clothes. The pale alien bared its teeth and plucked me from the stasis unit with a single hand around my throat. I tried to lift my hands to stop him, but he threw me negligently across the loading bay. I cried out when I slammed into the bulkhead.

"Ah, very good. I lost the first few batches, but I suppose the third time's the charm. I have a few more on their way too."

The man who spoke resembled the few pictures of Ximerans I'd seen. He was tall and muscular, with dark hair hanging to the middle of his back. His eyes were dark enough I couldn't discern pupils. A white scar marred the perfection of his face, and his full lips bowed up into a cruel smile as he looked down at me.

"So good of you to join me at last, Miss Andreyev. Would you care to tell me what animal shares your body?"

No shifter worth their fur would ever tell a stranger about their nature. Where had he gotten the information? "Animals are extinct on Earth. There aren't even any rats left."

"Come now, my dear. Let's not dissemble. Your genetics tell me that you shift your form into something with fangs and fur." He smirked as he sauntered toward me.

"Shall I take a guess? With that brindle hair, I bet you're a wolf."

He nudged me with the toe of his boot, prodding my hip painfully. "They are reputed to have been clever beasts and have the benefit of being small enough to manage." He kicked harder. "I confess that I'm glad you aren't a large cat or bear. While I would like one, I doubt my bed is big enough for their shifted forms."

I must not have done a good enough job hiding my expression. He laughed and pulled a black object from his pocket. "Don't worry. I have no interest in your animal in that way, nor would I trust a beast enough to allow her into my bed. Yet you're quite fetching in your human form."

He turned to two males standing behind him. "Stand her up and get her restrained. We'll see how many lashes she takes before she tells me what she is."

WHEN I WOKE, I was still naked except for metal cuffs on my wrists and ankles, and a collar around my neck, but I didn't worry about the shackles. The metal would fall away when we shifted.

They'd left me in a room bare of furnishings. The only things it held were a bowl of water and a thin blanket. I had no idea how they expected me to relieve myself, but that was the least of my worries.

My whole body ached like a bad tooth, courtesy of the Ximeran's vicious whip. Every time I moved another cut would open, seeping blood all over the floor. The wounds would heal if I could shift. Unfortunately, the tiger was somnolent; aware, but still shaking off the effects of the drugs I'd been given. There would be no help from the lazy thing. The door snicked open, and I heard male laughter. I turned my head toward the footsteps.

The Ximeran walked into the room, a tray in his outstretched hands. He set the tray down on the floor, and the foul smell of what he'd brought made my eyes water. "Eat, and then you may tell me what you are when you shift."

"Fuck you."

He had the whip out in a split second, and the fire of it stroked over my bare chest. I didn't have the breath to scream.

"I'd planned on letting you use your fingers." He grabbed my hair and pushed my face into the food. "But you're going to eat like an animal instead."

He held my face to the plate until I started to eat. Standing over me, he flicked that evil whip until I'd licked the last bit of disgusting sauce clean. I had no idea what the slop was. It was the most revolting thing I'd ever put in my mouth. My belly roiled, and I wondered if I would be sick.

I turned my face toward the Ximeran. If I was going to be sick, I was going to do it on the alien's legs.

"Good pet." He flicked the switch on the black device and collected the tray. As he left, he added, "We'll try again after you've had time to think about your situation." The door shut behind him, and I heard a beep as it locked.

The tiger stretched and yawned widely. I let her take over. I don't know if it was the food, or the pain, or if my captors finally decided I was cowed enough that they let the drugs wear off. A human would have died of blood loss or internal injuries. The lash had severed several nerves as well, and my body ached as the tiger attempted to regenerate them. Unfortunately, we couldn't heal much without shifting.

An alarm sounded when the shackles fell away, and the mist concealing our shift cleared. We were six hundred pounds of pissed-off. And we were hungry.

The door was automatic and refused to open for us, but it was a matter of just a moment to wedge a claw into the seam and wrench it away from the wall. Sparks flew from the destroyed wires and circuits. We ignored them and padded away from our prison.

There's nothing better than hearing the dying screams of enemies. We wanted to play, but we knew the treachery of these creatures. We killed without mercy, losing count after the first dozen or so. Blood, thick and black, sprayed over metal bulkheads and walls. It ran in slow streams toward drains. Ximerans and other things we didn't recognize fought beside the tall, pale creatures who had taken us.

A few had weapons that singed our fur and opened new wounds. One blast caught us in a haunch, cutting the flesh almost to the bone. We ignored the hurt, although it made us slow and vulnerable.

There was one left. We smelled him—our tormentor. He would die slow and hard. But he was running toward the loading bay, and we heard a digitized voice count down a shuttle launch. He would not escape us! We leaped forward and started running, reaching the loading bay just as he climbed into the shuttle.

He turned to us, fear and rage on his face as he snarled. "Fucking tiger!" he hissed. He turned away and almost made it into the shuttle.

Hot blood flowed down our throat as we took his leg, but he made it inside and sealed the door. Alarms blared, signaling his imminent escape. With a roar of disappointment, we snatched up the severed limb and raced away, rolling under the bulkhead door as it slammed shut.

We had a small trophy, but it would never be enough to satisfy us.

A dismembered head rolled into our path as we stalked through the corridors, our tail lashing angrily behind us. We batted it away and watched in satisfaction as it crashed against the wall and landed with a wet thud on the metal deck plate.

Yet there was something else. Our lips pulled back into a snarl as we tasted the air. One of the aliens who had taken us was still alive. And it was hiding not very far ahead. We dropped our prize and followed the scent, our paws silent on the metal floor.

The smell of delicious fear met our nose as we ripped the door to the storage cabinet away. The alien cried out when we snapped our jaws around its neck.

"Mercy! Please! We didn't—"

We tightened our jaws, stopping its speech as we dragged it from its hiding place. We let go of its neck only long enough to sever its right leg above the knee, spitting out the offensive flesh. It healed almost immediately, scabbing over with hardened tissue to cover the stump. Stupid aliens. Humans would bleed out quickly from such a wound, yet it would entertain us for much longer this way.

We cocked our head as it tried to scrabble away, its cries for mercy ignored. Another snap of our jaws took the left leg, and two more removed its arms above the elbows.

We used a paw to flip it to its belly and picked it up by the back of its neck in a prey drag back to our den. We would play and torment the limbless creature until...

My tiger chuffed and pushed me away as I tried to regain control of our body. We'd killed every living creature on the ship, but someone needed to fly it to Ximera. The tiger gave a mental shove hard enough to send me reeling, refusing to let go.

We arched our back into a play bow as the creature tried to scuttle away from us, using its abdominal muscles to creep along the floor. A bat of our paw sent it spinning into the metal wall. Blood trickled from its ear, and we huffed in disappointment when it lost consciousness.

But there was food to be had out there in the corridors. Vile as it was, we needed to eat.

CHAPTER

THREE

RAKON

I paced with worry as we approached the disabled luxury transport. The vessel had power and lights, but aside from the action of automatic stabilizers, it was still. Life support would be functional, but I didn't know if there was anything alive on board.

We'd gotten no distress call from the vessel. The sighting had been called in by one of the smugglers we had searching the system. Something was wrong on that transport. I felt it, and no one answered our attempts at communication.

"Get a dock on that tub. I want an armed boarding party ready to enter."

"Yes, Commander." My helmsman got to work, and I left the bridge to get ready for whatever we would find.

I don't think I've ever seen so much blood in one place. Not even during battle. The whole loading dock was covered with red gore and body parts. I swallowed hard as the scent of rot filled my nose. Whatever had happened hadn't been pretty. It was one thing to kill in battle, but I had a hard time making sense of what I was seeing. Whole skeletons rested in a corner, stripped of flesh as if they'd been chewed. I realized that was exactly what I was looking at when I found a long bone split and drained of marrow.

One of my males, a hardened soldier and veteran of many sorties, retched. I had to swallow and look away before I joined him in the act of expelling our last meals. A flash of movement caught my eye. Black-and-white stripes against dull metal. The creature used shadow and light for camouflage, but it was massive. It disappeared into the corridor, the black tip of a tail beckoning me to follow.

The corridors leading to the bridge weren't any better. I gave up trying to count limbs and just counted heads. Whatever had gotten to these males had torn them to pieces before consuming them. By their garments, I recognized a few Krenions, several Mendarans, and to my disgust, Ximerans. The Krenion bodies were the only ones that hadn't been consumed. Apparently, the creature hadn't liked the taste.

Doors had been ripped away from walls, allowing the thing access. Whatever the creature was, it was not humanoid and didn't appear to have the patience for control panels. We reached the bridge without incident.

I heard chuffing breaths and powered up my blaster. This creature had killed and consumed an entire crew. If this was the ship that had taken Renata, I wasn't sorry to see them dead, but when the creature opened its mouth into a snarl, I decided it needed to be put down. I just prayed it hadn't hurt her.

It stepped into the light and several of my males gasped. I heard blasters powering up behind me. The thing was massive, easily three meters long and a meter tall. My parents had given me a small shuttle when I'd been very young and just learning to fly. I thought it was about the same size.

It yawned and sat down by the captain's chair, its tail wrapped around huge paws tipped with wicked claws as it cocked its head at me. It was strangely beautiful, and I stared at it in fascination. It was heavily furred with black-and-white stripes, making me think it originated in a cold environment. Small, tufted ears pricked, and its mouth opened once more into a toothy yawn before it padded toward me.

I raised my blaster, hoping I had enough charge to kill it.

"Commander, wait!"

I stilled at my science officer's panicked words.

"*Panthera tigris altacia*. Give me a second, sir." He tapped furiously at his comm, and I wondered what he was up to. We were running out of time. Panthera whatever was stalking me, its nose working furiously. I backed away from the fangs, knowing it wasn't an appropriate maneuver for a Warlord. Those teeth were easily six Earth inches in length.

"Hold the fuck still, Commander!"

"Excuse me?" Mortal danger or not, I was not about to allow a subordinate to address me that way.

"Prey drive. If you run, she will chase, and you won't win. Sir."

"She?"

"No balls. She's a female." He smirked and turned his attention back to his comm as he slowly backed away. I matched his pace.

"Oh fuck no. She's heading for you, sir." He pulled his blaster from its holster. "With all due respect, Commander, I'll wait until her belly is full and try to hide."

Hot breath seared through the fabric of my uniform as the Panthera creature circled me. I shuddered as she twined her furry body around my legs. A low rumbling sounded from her throat.

"Is she going to eat me?"

"Checking, sir."

"Now would be a good time, Science Officer Patrek." The Panthera thrust her nose into my groin, and I heard the breath rasp in her throat as she rubbed her jaw against my cock. She moved around me, rubbing her face against my chest and arms. I heard her low rumbling. Despite my fear, the sound was... comforting.

Patrek chuckled. "No, as long as you stay still, I don't think she'll hurt you."

"Why not?"

"She's marking you as hers. Cats have scent glands in their face. They rub against things they consider theirs. I hope your house allows pets."

"You're an asshole, Science Officer Patrek."

"I know. If you can get a bit of her fur, I'd love a DNA sample. The Siberian Tiger is supposed to be extinct on Earth."

A rough tongue swiped across my hand as strong jaws closed around it. Though her teeth didn't break the skin, she tugged me forward until I had no choice but to follow. She let me go after a few steps, trusting that I'd keep up as she led me into a darkened chamber. It was a standard commercial transport chamber containing a bed and table. But there was one thing that wasn't standard.

"Mercy, Warlord. Please."

The whispered pleas of the thing on the floor didn't register at first. I stared at *Panthera Tigris Altacia* as she placed a serving platter-sized paw on the Krenion's torso. She chuffed and nudged the thing toward me.

"She's giving you a gift, Commander." I understood the intent of the words but couldn't fathom their meaning. A few taps on a comm sounded behind me. "When a cat thinks you can't provide for yourself, they'll bring you live prey."

Well, that was more than a little insulting. "What do I do?"

"Accept it. Kill it and eat it."

It would be a simple matter to twist the Krenion's neck. The snap of his vertebrae would be satisfying. But to eat?

The tiger staring into my eyes had other ideas. She swiped a paw down the Krenion's chest, opening his torso from neck to groin, exposing viscera as he screamed in agony. I kept my focus on those blue eyes. I'd seen them before. The pupils were elongated into ovals, just like... Renata's.

"I think I know what the extra chromosome in Renata and the other missing females is for."

"Sir?"

I waved my hand toward the tiger nosing around me. It was surprisingly comfortable to see her accept my presence enough to explore. "Science Officer Patrek, I think I'm presenting my genetic mate, Renata Andreyev."

He gave me an incredulous stare and chuckled as he crouched to pluck one of Renata's white hairs from the door frame. With a grunt, he turned and set it on the small table. "We'll see what the genetic analysis says, sir."

He looked down at his comm as a laser shot out, disintegrating the hair in a tiny puff of smoke and ash. He read over the display, his expression avid as results began streaming from the device. His face pale with wonder, Patrek looked up. "I don't know how it's possible, but that is the Andreyev female."

"I thought so."

"How did you know?" Patrek asked.

"Their eyes are the exact same. Type and cross match the samples from Chen Daiyu and Soledad Martinez, please. Try to match them with known Earth megafauna and get me the results before we reach Ximera."

"What do you think they are, sir?"

"No idea. I suggest you start with large predators. I'd begin looking at their originating continents to narrow it down."

He sighed heavily. "I don't even know where to start."

"Figure it out. You're dismissed."

When the door shut behind him, I knelt and laid my hand over her paw. "Shift now, Renata. You're safe."

RENATA

After one good whiff of Rakon, my tiger forgot her disgust, rolled to her back, and accepted him. The male to whom we'd given our last food was our mate and ordered us to shift. We should have kept one of the others for him. The skinny alien wasn't palatable.

I shouldn't have let him see me like this. I'd given away my greatest secret for... what? I was ashamed he'd seen me so weak that I was unable to regain control over the tiger.

"Shift, Renata." His whisper made the tiger arch as his hand found our spine, caressing the base of our tail. We wrapped the appendage around him, all four feet of it. We were ten feet, nose to tail. Six hundred pounds of fur, muscle, and claw. Yet we were like a cub under his searching fingers. It felt so damned good.

But we couldn't shift. The scent of blood was strong in our nose. Coupled with the scent of mate, it was too much. The tiger refused, baring fangs in protest, but our mate seemed to understand.

"Come, Renata. I'll take you someplace safe and clean." When we protested leaving our food, he snapped his fingers imperiously and nearly lost his hand for his temerity. Mate or not, we would tolerate no disrespect. We lowered our head to finish our meal.

He sighed and knelt. "I'm sorry, *penaka*. You can't kill him."

We growled low, not liking the idea of being denied our kill. The sound cut off when he laid a gentle hand on our muzzle, scratching the space between our eyes.

"We need him alive long enough to tell us what he knows about four more missing females and who hired him to take you." He leaned forward, touching his forehead to ours. "I promise you can have him back when we're done questioning him."

We lowered our head in acquiescence, ignoring the whimpers from our half-dead prey. He must have understood because he jerked his head at two other Ximerans behind him.

"Get that thing to medical and try to keep him alive long enough for questioning."

Though we weren't happy, we allowed them to take our kill. The small part of us that retained higher reason knew his words made sense. That thing most likely knew why we'd been taken. If not why, it knew who had given the order. We'd never caught the name of the Ximeran who escaped, but we had the piece of him we'd bitten off. Maybe Rakon would like it as a mating gift. It had aged just enough to make it smell delicious.

We nosed in the bedding we'd piled into a nest and pulled out the Ximeran's leg, then dropped it at our mate's feet. I would have to convince the tiger to shift before I could tell him what it meant.

He stopped and whispered to a potential prey. We couldn't understand what was said, but the other male grimaced and nodded, then picked up the leg and rushed into the new ship. Our mate rested a hand on our back, and we walked next to him as he led us into the new place. The metal corridors were empty, and we calmed as he led us into a spacious chamber.

The space was airy and open, not at all the same as the room in the other place. The air wasn't stale, reeking of old blood and filth. It was big enough for the tiger and had enough cover that we could den. Best of all, it smelled like our mate. We heard the sound of water and turned to watch him.

I'd never smelled anything so good as the fresh water he poured into a basin. It wasn't stale or boiled like we were used to. We padded forward when he set the basin on the floor. We bent our head down, and the single touch of our tongue to the effervescent fluid made us sneeze.

Yet it was so good. We lowered our head to the basin once more, emptying it with our cupped tongue. Our mate chuckled and poured more. We were desperately thirsty.

One of the prey tapped on the door frame. "Science Officer Patrek sent me to tell you *Panthera tigris* likes water, Commander. He says he's set the holo to simulate her natural environment."

"Thank you. Find her something clean to eat. I'd prefer it not be alive, but I'll take what I can get. I'm not having any luck convincing her to shift."

"Is this... normal?" The male swallowed and jerked his chin toward us.

"I have no idea. And find her something to wear on the off chance I manage to convince her to return to her human body. You can leave it in the holo near the door."

"Yes, Commander." He hurried away, leaving us alone with our mate.

He turned to us and asked, "Now that you've thoroughly terrified my crew, would you like a swim, Renata?"

The human part of us had never seen a body of water large enough or clean enough for swimming. Neither had the tiger, but she chuffed agreeably, and we padded forward, our tail swishing behind us. A crash sounded, and we leaped sideways into the corridor as the sound of our mate's laughter followed us.

He picked up several items that we'd knocked off a table in our haste to leave. "I think that will remind me to pick up after myself. That tail of yours is good at clearing the furniture."

The human part of us wanted to be embarrassed. We'd never shifted inside before. The tiger didn't care. She decided it was right that our mate cater to our whims.

Still chuckling, he moved into the corridor next to us and laid a palm on a panel next to the door. It slid shut without a sound.

"When you shift to your human form, we'll have the doors programmed to accept your touch. You'll be able to go anywhere you like on my ship, except for propulsion and the bridge." We followed him, the words only half registering as we took note of the locations of several prey following discreetly behind us.

"Actually, you can go both those places with an escort. Just ask if you have the interest, and I'll give you a tour." He glanced down at me. "Propulsion is a little too cramped to be comfortable for you right now, but I'm sure we could find space for you on the bridge if you watch where you put your tail."

We chuffed agreeably as he continued to point out features on the ship as we passed the galley, head, and a gym. We didn't know what the words meant, but our nose told us their purpose. We eventually reached a large metal door secured with another control panel. He placed his palm on the screen, and an electronic voice said, "Program Renata in process. Enter at your convenience, Commander."

The door slid open, and we stepped into wonderland.

FOUR

RAKON

Renata stilled as she took in the sight in front of her. I wished I could give her this on her home planet, but there was a similar environment on Ximera. The high meadows of Ximera's mountains were close enough to home we could travel there every weekend if she wanted. I owned a small cottage in one such place just a short flight from the city.

But fuck, it was cold. She didn't seem to notice the temperature, but she was in fur. I wondered if her human form was similarly impervious. Her massive paws were soundless on the leaf litter, and I watched as she disappeared into the dappled forest. Her stripes were the best camouflage I'd ever seen. I caught flashes of a black-tipped tail as I trudged along behind her.

She went still and dropped into a crouch. I looked ahead and spotted a holographic deer browsing through the trees. It wasn't alive and wouldn't have a fear response. Well, it might, depending on how thorough Patrek had been when he'd programmed this sim. I held my breath as I watched Renata stalk the creature.

She twined her body through the sun-dappled forest, breath-taking and silent as she crept forward a few feet at a time. The deer startled and tried to run just as she rose up and sprang, her powerful haunches launching her through the air. She brought the animal down, her jaws clamped around its throat.

I laughed at her angry roar of disappointment when the creature vanished, but pressed my lips together to cut it off when she growled at me. She trotted back, her twitching tail the only sign of her irritation. She was not a happy kitty.

"I'm sorry. It didn't occur to me that Science Officer Patrek would have time to program in fauna or I would have warned you. Would you like to help me find the lake so you can have your swim?"

She bared her teeth at me, but turned away, trotting forward purposefully as if she knew where she was going. I realized she probably had a better sense of smell and could scent water. How much of her instincts and senses did she retain as a human? I sighed and trudged behind her, knowing I had a lot to learn about my new mate.

Within a few minutes, she led me straight to a massive lake. Snowcapped peaks were reflected in the mirrorlike surface, and she stopped at the sandy shore, looking down into the water. I wondered if she regarded her own reflection. Had she never seen how magnificent she was? Given the state of her home planet, it was certainly possible.

She suddenly darted forward, her powerful hind legs sending her soaring over the water. She landed with a tremendous splash, the water casting rainbows in the sun. I settled to my haunches to watch her play, hoping this would be enough to make her shift. I was growing tired of our one-sided conversation, and I wanted to hear her speak. I already knew what she looked like, but I needed to see for myself that she was uninjured.

I wished I could swim with her, but Ximeran bodies weren't designed for immersion in cold water. I admitted to a little jealousy though. The splashing stopped, and she swam to shore, leaving only faint ripples to mark her passage.

She padded from the water and stood dripping in front of me. Her head turned side to side, slowly at first, but picking up speed as the shake traveled down her body. Her tongue lolled out between daggerlike fangs as I wiped the frigid water from my face.

"I suppose that's my penance for not telling you about the deer."

She panted heavily and dropped to the sand, rolling to her back as she squeezed the last of the water from her fur. Standing, she shook once more, sending wet sand flying. I moved back when I saw the telltale head movement.

The air shimmered around her as she walked toward me, and I couldn't understand what I was seeing. It looked like fog, but Patrek wouldn't have programmed fog on a sunny day. I rubbed my eyes as I tried to catch sight of her.

The fog dissipated, and she touched my face, her callused fingertips rough on my skin. I laid my palm over her hand, relishing our first contact as I looked down into her beautiful blue eyes. Alien eyes, but all the more striking for it.

"I'm glad to meet you, Miss Andreyev." I stepped back, keeping hold of her hand. She was more beautiful than the lackluster photo I'd seen on my comm. A faint dappling of stripes was on her cheeks, but they faded as I watched, her tiger going dormant.

"I'm glad to meet you as well, Warlord Rakon. Or is it Commander?" Her lips curled into a grin, and I had to smile back.

"You call me Rakon. Or mate. Or whatever you want. Everyone else calls me Commander."

She laughed, and I took a moment to study her body. I'd been mostly successful keeping my eyes up. Even with my admittedly limited experience with females who were not paid courtesans, I knew no woman wanted to be ogled. She was my mate, not a collection of body parts, but I couldn't help myself.

By all the ancient gods, she was gorgeous. Nearly as tall as a Ximeran female would have been, her chin was level with my shoulder. Surprisingly, her bicolored hair was dry and hung past her shoulders in a tangled curtain. Her lips were full, and I could picture them wrapped around my cock. The image was so enticing that I hardened in my trousers.

Shadows concealed her too-thin body, but her pink nipples hardened under my gaze. Although she lacked the ample flesh possessed by most Ximeran females, her curves were glorious. Her long legs were corded with muscle, and I loved the understated ridges of her abdomen. She was spectacular, and I growled as I imagined her at a healthy body weight. Other males would want her, and that would not be tolerated.

She stepped out of the shadows, and I gasped in horror as I examined her. Heavy scarring decorated her torso, some of the wounds red and seeping blood. I spun her around, ignoring her irritated huff. I didn't see how it was possible, but her back was worse, and there was a partially healed blaster wound on her hip. How was she even standing?

"Fuck, Renata! What happened to you?" I swept her up into my arms, clutching her tightly as I raced back to the holo entrance. "End sim. Science officer to medical immediately. Medic Krenak to medical right fucking now!"

"Rakon—"

"Get me Council on vid and feed it to medical."

"Rakon, wait—"

"And someone get the Earth liaison on vid. I want to talk to him, too."

RENATA

"Rakon!"

He finally stopped, blinking down at me in surprise. I knew what the wounds looked like, and his reaction wasn't at all out of line.

"They'll heal a little more every time I shift. Don't worry about it. They'd be healed already, but I kind of..." Ugh. I did not want to tell my beautiful mate that I'd lost control of the tiger for weeks. How embarrassing!

"You're going to medical right now. I won't have you in pain, and I don't care about anything else." He squeezed me tighter, nearly pushing the breath from my lungs. "Besides, if you could have healed them yourself, you would have done it already."

His stern gaze met mine, and I squirmed. "Well, about that..." I paused, casting about for words that wouldn't make me look like a weak fool. "You see, I—"

"Spit it out, mate."

I couldn't help the shiver that coursed down my spine at his low growl. Our mate would make a most excellent tiger. "Pain and stress sometimes make my tiger..." I looked down, unwilling to meet his eyes, but he tipped my chin up.

"Now, Renata, before I lose patience."

"I lost control, okay?" I think my shout surprised both of us. He nearly dropped me. "Pain and stress make the tiger nearly impossible to control, and I was too weak to keep her from taking over."

Tears pricked my eyes, and I jerked my chin away from his grasp, lowering my head so he wouldn't see me cry.

"*Penaka*, look at me."

I refused and he used a thumb to wipe away my tears before he gripped my chin. His grasp wasn't hard enough to hurt me, but he wasn't having my disobedience. I opened my eyes to find him staring at me, his eyes filled with sympathy and fierce retribution.

"I'm very proud of you, little *penaka*. You did what was necessary to protect yourself, and I couldn't ask for a better mate. You're the perfect match for a Warlord."

I stilled as he brushed a soft kiss over my lips. "Now, let's get you to medical. Do you remember what was used to hurt you?"

Although I'd had sex partners before, no one had ever kissed me. The sensation made my core clench in desire, and I wished he would do it again. The scent and taste of him drove everything else out of my head. He was like I imagined honey would be, sweet and delicious.

"Renata? Do you remember?" he asked again.

I shook my head and focused on the conversation, grateful he couldn't smell my sudden arousal. "Yes, but I don't know what it's called. It was a black device that had a switch. The lash was like a bolt of lightning."

He winced, and his strides quickened. "No wonder you aren't healing. I've never seen one in person because laser whips are illegal in all known sectors."

"I doubt carrying contraband is the greatest of that male's crimes." I'd meant the comment to be funny, but Rakon's face darkened into a scowl.

"No. Krenion are supposed to be extinct. They—" His words cut off as we reached an open room filled with the smell of disinfectant coupled with the faint odor of the Krenion who had kidnapped me. My lips pulled back in an atavistic snarl.

The prey that accompanied Rakon during my rescue came forward with a blanket. He tucked it around me and patted my cheek fondly, earning himself a growl from my mate.

"If the Krenion dies, I will send the entire medical staff to sector nineteen. He's going to tell us everything we want to know about who hired him to take my mate, and then I'm going to let her eat him."

The acrid scent of terror was delicious. One of the crew members even let out a small trickle of urine, and I smiled as I tucked my face against my mate's chest. I had so many questions, and I needed to tell them what I knew of the Ximeran who had taken me, but it could wait. The tiger butted gently against me, encouraging me to bite and stake my claim on my male. I pushed her away. That was a conversation for another time when Rakon wasn't quite so angry.

"What do we have here, Rakon? Did your little mutant get a hangnail?"

The voice was feminine and sultry, and my eyes narrowed at the hot gaze the strange female leveled at my mate. She had amber eyes set in a round face, with light brown hair curling down her back in neat ringlets. Although she was taller than me and well nourished, she was soft. We would kill her easily.

To his credit, Rakon only sighed and rolled his eyes. "Do you not pay attention to anything, Medic Merkella? This is War Mate Renata, my genetic mate."

"No. Only what I can see with my own eyes... Rakon. And all I see is a zoo specimen." Her eyes trailed down to my mate's groin, and I had to struggle hard to keep the tiger from ripping her face off.

Rakon set me down on my feet, and I started toward her. "Two rules, *penaka*. You can't shift, and you can't kill her. She's one of only a few dozen female Ximerans."

I decided to ask what happened to the rest of them another time. "What is that word you call me?"

The female answered before Rakon could speak. "It's a furry creature we often keep as pets. Useless little things, really, just like you." She sauntered forward and pushed me aside to run a possessive hand down my mate's chest. He scowled and moved around her to take my arm.

Claws snapped from my fingers and toes, and stripes formed on my body as the tiger struggled to break free. "If I could shift, she'd shit herself, and I wouldn't have to hurt her."

Nervous titters filled the room as the males backed away. "No shifting, Renata. Behave yourself."

"Spoilsport." I ignored his laughter and advanced on the female Ximeran. She sneered at me and pulled a curved dagger, slashing it forward and catching the skin of my belly before I could leap away.

"Stand still, mutant. Rakon is mine, and all I have to do is kill you."

My fangs dropped, and I had to forcibly push my tiger back as I circled the Ximeran female. I was certain that Rakon's order was the

44

only reason the tiger hadn't burst forth. "Are you sure I can't kill her?"

"No, but she's likely to be arrested and sentenced to sector nineteen for trying to kill the mate of a Warlord."

"What is with you people?" I dodged another stab, then caught her hand and squeezed hard enough to make her drop the blade. When she screamed in pain, I realized I'd broken most of the bones in her hand, but I didn't let go. I'd gotten better fights from malnourished humans on Earth. "You get all pissy about a little good-natured killing, give me a deer that disappears when I catch it, and then I have to come into this place that reeks of disease and blood just to smack a bitch down."

The female's whimpers grew tiresome, and I realized she'd collapsed to her knees, her hand still clenched in my fist. It looked like fresh meat. I'd inadvertently pulverized the bones. Oh well. Most creatures did fine with only one hand.

"You wanted my mate bad enough that you were willing to pull a knife." I kicked her in the chest, my bare foot snapping ribs as she flew backward, landing with a sickening crunch against the wall. I wondered if I'd broken her back. "If you want him that badly, come try to take him."

But she didn't. Her eyes were glazed with pain, and she didn't have enough breath to whimper. I strode forward to haul her to her feet, but Rakon caught me in his arms before I could reach her. Two medics crouched next to her with instruments in their hands.

"She'll survive with proper treatment, Commander."

"Good. Once you've patched her up, have security escort her to confinement. She'll face charges when we return to Ximera."

He picked me up and set me on a table, then leaned his forehead against mine. "I'm proud of you, little *penaka*. You didn't shift, and you didn't kill her." He kissed me hard, leaving me breathless, but didn't give me time to enjoy it.

Straightening, he started barking orders, and I found myself surrounded by medics. One had a med injector, but I waved him away. He looked at Rakon with questions in his eyes. "It's just pain blocker, Commander. It will make her more comfortable while we treat her wounds."

"Ask Renata if you want permission. She's right there."

He flushed and turned to me, the injector at his side. "War Mate, this chemical will make the pain receptors in your body go dormant for a short time. It can't cause unconsciousness, nor will it keep you from moving."

"I see. How long does it last?"

"The dosage I've prepared, based on your apparent weight and assumed body fat, should only last an hour or two at most. It should be enough time for us to repair the damage, but you might feel some discomfort at the end."

I held out my arm. There was a bit of pressure and a hissed puff of air, but I didn't feel a thing. The pain of my wounds was almost immediately deadened. I'd made light of them for Rakon's sake, but they'd hurt like the devil.

"Speaking of body fat." The medic's tone was almost conversational. "Feed your mate, Warlord. You've let her get into an astonishingly bad condition." He blinked as he realized who he'd denigrated. "With all due respect, Commander."

When Rakon glared at him, I snorted in amusement. I liked this medic person. "What's your name?"

"Medic Krenak, War Mate."

"You can call me Renata."

He swallowed and lowered his head, focusing his attention on the long, seeping cut trailing over my left breast. "It wouldn't be appropriate. In your position, given names are only for mates."

"Oh. I see." It would have been nice for Rakon to share that little tidbit, but I supposed it hadn't come up. It made me doubly angry that the female I'd fought had used his name. I felt no guilt over her injuries. Perhaps the other females would learn from her lack of wisdom.

I looked down to watch Krenak work. The cuts disappeared

under his instrument, leaving behind faint pink scars. It was slow going though. I was already feeling twinges of pain from the wounds on my back. When he dug too hard at a wound on my thigh, I flinched.

Krenak lifted his hands and backed away. "I beg your pardon. May I give you another dose of pain blocker?"

"The sooner the better." It had lasted half as long as he'd said, but my body wasn't exactly typical. My shifter metabolism didn't allow foreign chemicals to hang around. I wondered what drug the alien had used. It had been very potent to knock a shifter unconscious.

"I've never seen wounds left from a laser whip," Krenak murmured. "It's no wonder they're illegal, but I have to wonder who managed to find one."

"The male who hurt me was Ximeran," I said.

"That isn't possible!" Rakon was clearly angry at my news, but I knew what I'd seen.

"If you don't believe me, check the DNA on the leg I gave you. Also, when you go looking for him, he has a long white scar from his left eye to the corner of his mouth, dark hair past his shoulders, and is missing his left leg above the knee. I can't imagine he'll be too hard to find."

We stared at each other, both of us angry, but he tore his gaze from mine and wiped a hand over his face, sighing deeply.

"The male you describe has been dead for almost fifteen cycles." His face softened. "I'm sorry, but it just isn't possible."

"Then forget the scar and look for a Ximeran with a missing leg. Check the DNA before you decide I'm lying because part of the male who hurt me is on this ship." I shrugged, trying to hide my irritation. "Besides, you know perfectly well there were other Ximerans on the transport. You would have found what was left of them."

Lying back on the med table, I waved at the medic to continue, trying to hold in my tears. Between being kidnapped and developing a healthy dislike of the arrogant asshole who genetics decided would be my mate, I just wanted to go back to Earth and forget the whole experience. But I couldn't. The male with the scar was still out there, and he'd mentioned taking other shifters. If my idiotic mate wouldn't help me, I'd do it myself.

Sighing heavily, Krenak finished his work on my back and helped me sit up, covering me with a blanket. "Take care of yourself, War Mate. You're shockingly durable, so the only medical advice I have is for you to eat and rest."

I didn't protest when Rakon swept me into his arms, the blanket wrapped snugly around my body. I couldn't wait to get some clothes, and despite my irritation with him, I loved feeling his warmth against my bare skin. I nuzzled him at the spot where his shoulder met his neck. I would set my bite to that place. Maybe. I still didn't know how he would react to what I had to tell him.

Given his uncompromising rigidity, I didn't think my news would go over well at all.

A wide yawn split my face, and I rested my head on his shoulder. Explanations would have to wait. My mate held me in his arms. His scent of musk and something astringent surrounded me, and I wanted nothing more than to burrow into our nest with him and wrap myself around his heated body.

CHAPTER

FIVE

RAKON

I had every intention of letting Renata rest without me pawing her. I had so many thoughts running through my head I knew I wouldn't sleep. I laid her on my bed, watching in amusement as she ripped the sheets free and piled them into the center. It was yet another reminder that my pretty mate was driven by instincts I didn't fully understand. When I bent to kiss her, she extended her claws and dug them into my arm. I winced at the pain, but she managed not to break the skin as she pulled me into the nest she'd made.

I let her wrap her body around mine, willing my hardened cock to behave itself. Now was not the time. My War Mate needed sleep and food, not necessarily in that order. I'd have liked to feed her before she slept, but she'd made the decision without my input. Stubborn female. I stroked her hair fondly. *My* stubborn female.

Her skin was so soft. I tucked a piece of hair behind her ear, marveling at the velvety texture. She grunted and nuzzled my chest, burying herself in my arms as she wrapped a strong thigh around my hips. I bit back a groan, knowing she was naked and completely open to me. Willing my cock to subside, I kissed the top of her head.

I also owed her an apology. She'd been right to remind me of the presence of Ximerans on the transport that had stolen her.

I didn't think it was coincidence that three of the five known shifter females had been matched with Warlords. Judging by Renata's destruction of the crew who had taken her, and her reaction to Merkella's unwise assumption that I would continue our dalliance, they would be ideal War Mates.

Fuck, just watching her fight had me hard as steel in my uniform. Part of me wanted to ignore her wounds and claim her right there in medical. Let everyone watch as I made her mine so no one would dispute my claim to her delectable body. I wanted my mark on her, wanted her to smell like me and know she was mine.

Yet I had to wonder. Renata's tiger was always present, always waiting for an opportunity to push through her defenses. I'd met a few humans. Even when she wore a human skin, the tiger wasn't far beneath the surface and marked her as different. I would never tell her, but I longed to see her human skin without the faint black stripes.

I turned over and closed my eyes as I tugged the bundle of warm female closer. She would adjust well to life on Ximera. She would be protected there and not have to live with the threat of starvation or injury. Maybe the stripes would fade if I could manage to make her feel safe.

I couldn't imagine what Ximeran would have taken her. We'd been certain Norkad had died when we blew up his ship as he tried to escape justice. He'd harmed so many when he decided that colluding with the Krenions would gain him power and wealth. Yet Renata had been sure the male who had hurt her had borne his distinctive scar. I should know it. I'd been there when Markon gave it to him.

We'd just have to test the remains. I doubted it would tell us the individual, but testing would tell us a species.

I reached over and tapped my comm, thumbing it to the cooks in the galley. "Set the replicator to produce deer meat."

"Sir?"

"As much as it will make before morning, and don't bother to cook it."

"Sir, what's a deer?"

"Have Science Officer Patrek assist. He knows what they are."

"Yes, Commander."

I touched the comm to end the communication and settled back into bed. Renata hadn't stirred. I hoped my gift would please her.

Closing my eyes, I tried to will my body to rest. Renata moved against me and, to my surprise, rumbled low in her throat like she'd done on the Mendaran cruiser. Whatever the sound was, it resonated with pleasure and comfort. Her fingers clenched and relaxed in the muscles of my chest; a repetitive motion that made no sense to me.

Shifting her weight, she pressed her damp core against my cock, and I groaned.

Her eyes opened at the sound.

"Am I disturbing you?" She gave me a naughty grin and wriggled against me.

"Go back to sleep, *penaka*."

"I'm not tired. And I want to—"

I reached around and slapped her ass, relishing the feel of her warm flesh as it bounced against my hand. She hissed and stared at me as her pupils dilated in arousal. "Go to sleep, Renata. Medic Krenak ordered you to rest."

Her eyes narrowed, the pupils elongating and narrowing as stripes danced across her face. "Maybe I should look for another male who will meet my needs."

In a flash, she was on her back. "You will not, mate." I nudged her thighs apart, settling between them as her wet heat soaked the front of my trousers. Holding her hands in one of mine, I slid down her body until my face was level with her wet pussy. Inhaling deeply, I growled. She smelled so damned good.

And then she lifted her hips, offering that beautiful cunt to me. I couldn't resist. No male could. I touched my tongue to a trickle of moisture escaping her pussy, enjoying the sweet, delicious taste of her. She whimpered, wordlessly asking for more. I gave it to her, stabbing my tongue deep inside her as I lapped up the taste of her pleasure.

The nub at the top of her sex needed attention too. I sucked that sweet little bit of hardened flesh into my mouth, watching as her eyes went wide. She opened her mouth, and her head fell back as she moaned in pleasure.

I liked seeing my mate's joy, but something was missing. Her pretty pussy was too empty. I worked a finger into her core, loving the feel of her muscles clenching down on me. Turning my hand, I sought out the roughened flesh deep within her I hoped would be there. It gave great pleasure to both Mendaran and Ximeran females.

To my delight, I found the right spot that would send my beautiful, fierce mate into rapture. Sucking her clit into my mouth, I pressed up against that telltale bit of flesh inside her. With a scream, she erupted for me, her gush of pleasure soaking my face, smelling of desire. Easing my finger from inside her, I licked her softly to ease her down and gathered every trace of her sweet essence.

Though I'd been with many other females, none tasted or smelled like Renata. She was singularly delicious. I rubbed my face against her pussy, bathing myself in her sticky, wet cum. I had no experience with humans though. If all of them were as delectable as she was, it was no wonder they were highly prized mates. Of course, maybe it was her Felidae nature, in which case, I counted myself the luckiest Warlord ever born.

I wanted to mark her with my scent, and it was disappointing that I didn't have the right physiology to rub pheromones all over her like she'd done to me on the Mendaran cruiser. Maybe she would accept a small chemical brand like the one designating my rank and family. But I wouldn't mark her velvety cheek. Her arm, perhaps, or the back of her hand.

She whimpered, her thighs clenching my head tightly before relaxing and falling open. The rumbling sound started again, and I let go of her hands. She relaxed as I crawled up and took her lips in a soft kiss, sharing the taste of her. It was all I could do to stop myself from fucking her. My balls ached with the need to spill inside her, and every bit of blood in my body filled my cock to bursting. Surreptitiously, I fisted my swollen flesh, willing it to obey and not spill inside my uniform pants. I refused to come unless I could do it inside her luscious body.

I pushed sweat-dampened hair away from her face and stared into her beautiful, drowsy eyes. She needed rest, not her future mate rutting on her like an untried youth. "Go to sleep, *penaka*."

RENATA

I stared at Rakon in shock, unsure of what I'd heard. Had he... turned me down? I knew I wasn't much to look at, and he was seeing me at my absolute worst, but I'd never once met a male who would refuse the offer of sex.

"But you didn't—"

"And I won't until you agree to be my mate in front of the Ximeran Council," he interrupted.

I growled at him before bucking hard enough to roll him to his back. Straddling his hips, I said, "I want to fuck now."

"Ah, there's my fierce tiger." He laughed and caught my hands before throwing me off him. I landed with a heavy thump on the other side of the bed. "It's time you learned that you aren't the apex predator anymore."

I screeched as he flipped me to my belly and restrained my hands with his belt. Still holding my wrists, his free hand crashed down on my bare ass. I tried to shift, but my tiger chuffed in amusement and curled in the back of our head to watch. Crazy beast. Of all the times to go against our nature and demand our due, she chose now to refuse my pleas for help.

Rakon peppered my backside with his hard hand, bringing a flush of warmth to my skin that somehow mutated into pleasure. It hurt, but felt good at the same time, and I was very confused. Although I'd had a few human lovers, none of them had ever spanked me before. I didn't know how to behave. The human part wanted to shift and bite off his hand for his behavior. Sort of, maybe we wanted to do that.

He stroked my ass, his hand warm and comforting, easing the sting of his blows. He spanked me again, a flurry of slaps to my upper thighs that made me squeal in pain. That fucking hurt, and he held me down when I tried to roll away.

Yet as he pushed down on my hips, my pussy ground against the bedding, sending a shockwave of heated sensation into my core. I closed my eyes and tried to bite back a whimper as he stroked my ass. But a needy whine escaped when he pushed his free hand between my legs and touched me. Rakon chuckled as he stroked my wet flesh, his fingers slipping easily between my damp folds.

"Maybe spanking you isn't going to work as punishment," he murmured, his fingers still busy between my legs. "Let's find out." He pulled his hand away and stood, leaving me helpless.

I could have gotten up. Maybe I could have broken the belt holding my wrists together. I could shift and escape him altogether. I did nothing except lie there and try to rub my cunt into the sheets as heat from my spanked ass warmed me, morphing from pain into something else.

He returned, standing over my prone body with one hand tucked behind his back. "Such a naughty kitty," he said. "I think we'll have to take away some temptation."

Without another word, he helped me to stand and bent me over the bed before kicking my feet apart. He pulled my hips back, removing the temptation to rub against the bed. Standing to my side, he rested a hand on my back. My breathing rasped in my throat as I arched into his touch. I wanted relief from the throbbing tension he'd built. I wanted his hands on me, his beautiful cock inside me. I ached to bite.

His hand fell on my exposed backside again and again, the flurry of spanks covering the globes of my ass. I screeched in pain, the sound morphing into my tiger's yowl. But the tiger wasn't screaming in pain or anger. It was all pleasure. He thrust his fingers inside me once more, as his thick thumb, wet with my juices, prodded at my anus.

Shit! I couldn't even get enough breath to cry out. He penetrated that virgin hole, just enough to open me, but not enough to hurt. I had no idea what to feel. It was good, so damned good, but I didn't know if it was wrong. My body stalled on that edge of cataclysmic pleasure as humiliation and want mixed into a maelstrom of need.

Too soon, he jerked away and set his wet hand to the tender skin where my ass met my thighs, his punishing blows making my flesh jiggle. And then he moved, and his hand caught my exposed pussy. My orgasm, stalled and hovering on the edges of consciousness, exploded and sent me spiraling into darkness. I clenched on air as my body pulsed with aftershocks and pain mixed with wet pleasure clouded my vision.

From a million miles away, he said, "I can keep spanking you, or you can behave yourself and wait until we're properly mated. Which is it going to be?"

Allowing my body to go limp under his touch, I panted, trying to regain my breath before I could speak. "Fine. No sex until we're mated."

"There's a good tiger." He loosened the bonds trapping my wrists and picked me up. Settling me next to him on the bed, he tapped my nose, then pulled me into his arms. "We'll discuss our mating in the morning after you've rested."

My tiger purred with amusement. *Bit off more than you could chew, didn't you?*

"Oh, shut up."

Despite the need raging through my body, my tiger's lulling purr sent me to sleep.

RAKON

I woke to an empty bed. Renata's carefully constructed nest was scattered on the floor, and I shivered, missing her warmth and her wild scent, like the wind off the glaciers in Ximera's southern seas. Unfortunately, I heard footsteps in the main room of my quarters. With a heavy sigh, I crawled off the bed and tugged on pants. I hadn't gotten much sleep, but I was delighted Renata had slept through the night. Maybe today she'd be calm enough I could see her without the ever-present stripes.

"Commander Rakon!"

The steward's panicked voice reached me through the thin door, and I sighed. Renata was terrifying my crew. Again. It was a shame Merkella hadn't paid attention. She might still have her hand and not be on her way to sector nineteen. I opened the door, dreading what I would see.

Renata was shifted, and her tiger twined around the steward's legs as he held a heavy tray above his head. His panicked expression made me want to laugh, but I held it in. She rumbled loudly. I didn't know what the sound was called, but I fucking loved it. That throaty vibration made my cock hard every time I heard it.

"She knows you have her breakfast. Set it down for her."

"But I—"

"She won't hurt you. Just put the tray on the floor." Turning my attention to the tiger, I said, "Renata, leave my steward alone. He can't set the tray down with you hovering like that."

She chuffed irritably but backed away and sat on her haunches, wrapping her long tail around her feet. She looked almost... prim, but the deep rumbling in her throat didn't stop as she watched the steward set the tray on the floor. He backed away slowly, his empty hands held out in front of him as he made his escape.

She was eating before the steward left, that delicious rumbling only stopping when she swallowed. It was replicated meat, but she didn't seem to care. Her obvious enjoyment made me wonder what she'd eaten on Earth. Her meal didn't last long, and she licked the plate clean before looking around for more.

"I'm sorry. We'll have more for you tomorrow." The air shimmered over her, signaling her shift. I wished I could see it.

"It's okay. I'm sorry I scared him, but I smelled the meat and..." She grimaced and shrugged, the faded stripes on her face turning pink with embarrassment.

"How long have you been on the edge of starvation, Renata?"

Her flush deepened, and she looked at the floor, her hands clenching. "I'm not."

"Don't lie." She flinched at my harsh tone, but I wouldn't take the words back. She would have to learn that I intended to make her healthy and happy. Not necessarily in that order, but both would happen if I had to paddle her ass to get it done.

"You were too skinny in the image that came with your genetic profile. You're still too thin. Now answer the question."

She glared at me, her hands still clenched at her sides. I grabbed a blanket off the sofa and threw it over her shoulders. Where were her fucking clothes? I couldn't yell at her if she was naked.

"I had more to eat than most."

She looked so proud and determined as she defended herself against my question. I pulled her into my arms and nuzzled my face into her sweetly scented hair. "That's not what I asked, and there's no shame in admitting it. How long have you been hungry?"

She sighed and relaxed against me. "Forever, okay? It's been forever."

"You won't have to do it again. It's not perfect, but the replicator can make anything you want. And when we get to Ximera, you'll be able to hunt."

"Anything I want?" Her eyes brightened, and she looked up at me.

"If it's in a database that Science Officer Patrek can find, we can make it."

"I want fish. My friend Sendra told me about it once, but I've never seen one. She was alive when the storms came, but she's gone now."

Her face tightened and she sniffed. I realized her friend must have died recently. I pulled her into my arms and kissed her. "I'm sorry for your loss. We'll get your fish after we find you some clothes."

"The steward brought some. Give me a minute and I'll be ready." I let her go and watched as she bent over a pile of fabric on the floor. A standard uniform shirt went over her head, hiding her magnificent breasts. She turned around to stuff her legs into the pants, and I noticed the scars were almost completely gone. She'd been telling the truth. With enough shifts, she'd have healed on her own, but I was glad I'd insisted on medical attention.

She took my hand as I led her toward my pride and joy. I was the only Warlord with his own aquarium set up in an empty storage room. It wasn't big enough for fishing, of course, but the fish were all food species, and we occasionally caught one to share when we got hungry for something fresh.

She bent down to look into the water, her expression entranced as she watched the fish dart around. There were a few big ones that might be ready for...

In a flash, she had one of the largest out of the water. It flopped on the deck, giving her a baleful stare. She shifted and had the creature devoured within a few seconds as I stared in shock. When she coughed out the tail, I burst out laughing.

She regained her human form, her face red. "I am so sorry! Was it a pet?" Refusing to meet my eyes, she tugged her clothes over her body once more.

"No. It wasn't a pet, but you should wait until we reach Ximera. The crew likes to feed them, and there are many places you can fish."

"I feel terrible." Her clawed hands covered her face, and I wondered when she'd realize the tiger still rode her hard.

"Was it good?"

A shy, beautiful smile lit her face, and I thought my heart would stop at the sight. "It was the best thing I've ever eaten."

I chuckled and pulled her to my chest as I dropped a kiss into her hair. My mate was so damned cute. I just hoped we could muddle through our cultural differences and make things work. And I prayed to all the old gods the Ximeran people would accept her and the other unusual females we'd identified.

I prayed there were more than just those five.

RENATA

There were several problems with my situation. First, I'd demanded sex from Rakon, knowing I risked giving him my bite without his permission. My ass still burned from his hard hand, an aching, delicious sting. I was wet just thinking about his mastery over me and my tiger. It was clear she'd accepted Rakon, otherwise she'd have allowed us to shift. And the pleasure he'd given me. Heat rose in my pussy just thinking about it.

And then we'd eaten his fish.

I couldn't believe I'd done that! What the fuck was wrong with me? It was one thing to terrify Rakon's steward into dropping that tray filled with rich, meaty goodness. No. I had to murder one of his pet fish.

He'd said it wasn't a pet, but I didn't believe him. When a person feeds an animal, they are by definition, keeping a pet. And we ate it. I wanted to crawl in a hole and die of embarrassment.

Stupid damned cat. Stupid instincts. Stupid me. The tiger showed me her teeth, utterly unrepentant. She'd liked the fish and would do it again. I coughed into my hand and scowled when I produced another fishbone.

I wanted to hurt someone when Rakon laughed at me. "Oh, *penaka*, don't be so hard on yourself. It is a proven fact that all beings are food aggressive when they've experienced starvation. I know of several examples." He waved his hands expansively as he led me to his quarters.

"Your Earth right now, and several times in the past. Sector twelve just got through a devastating drought. We've spent the last year hauling food and water to the needy, and they're all like you are. You just..." He flushed and scrubbed at his face. "You're just a little more obvious about it."

"It doesn't make eating your fish right." I had no idea why he was being so understanding. If it were me, I'd have kicked my ass to the curb.

He stopped, pulling me against his chest. "It doesn't make it wrong. It just is." His lips came down on mine, and I lost myself in his searing kiss right there in the corridor. I relished the taste of him, caressing his tiny incisors with my tongue as I wished they were tiger fangs. I would have kept right on kissing him, but a throat clearing behind us interrupted our moment.

Rakon sucked my lower lip, but let it go with a sigh. "Patrek, this had better be important."

"Yes, Commander. I have Council on the comm. They wish to speak with you about War Mate Renata."

"About what?"

The other male scowled. "Apparently, someone has been carrying tales, sir. They wish to address her attack on a Ximeran female."

"I beg your pardon?"

"Merkella got hold of someone's comm and used it to tell the Council that the War Mate attacked her without provocation."

"Who did the comm belong to?"

"It was Krenak's. She must have taken it when he was in confinement to treat her injuries. He's not very happy."

"Have him meet me on the bridge, along with the other witnesses."

Patrek smirked. "He's already up there. His father is on the Council, and the last I saw he was tearing into the old fuck."

Rakon laughed, but I didn't see what was so funny. I knew about such things. Xenophobia would make sure I didn't get fair treatment over one of their women, no matter who started the fight. Well, I wasn't on Ximera yet. If they made a decision I didn't like, I would make Rakon take me back to Earth and have the humans remove my sample from the database.

It meant that I wouldn't be able to help locate other shifters, but maybe I could do that on my own. I could at least search my home region before I starved.

"Escort Renata to my quarters and meet me on the bridge."

"Yes, sir." Patrek held out a hand. "If you'll follow me, War Mate?"

"No. I want to come with you." I clutched at Rakon's arm. My claws came out, and I forced them back, reminding myself I didn't need them to hold on.

He stared at me thoughtfully, watching as my claws receded. "Are you sure, *penaka*? They're likely to make you angry, and your control is... Well, less than perfect when you're irritated."

"I have to try. If I don't stand up for myself now, I won't get any respect in the future."

"The War Mate has a point, sir. You know how they are," Patrek said. I had to remind myself that he was no longer prey. He'd given me the lovely lake and food.

"I don't know..." Rakon rubbed his chin, the short hair on his jaw rasping against his palm as he stared down at me. "Do you think you can keep your tiger under wraps no matter what? They will be nasty and rude to you."

"They're nasty and rude to everybody though," Patrek added. "Personally, I can't wait to see you shift in front of them. It might teach them humility."

Rakon rolled his eyes and scowled at the other male. "That's true, but it's not nice to say." He smirked wickedly. "Imagine what they'd do if they saw what she left on that Mendaran transport." Shaking his head, he added, "You should have heard her roar on the holo. I'd give anything to be able to do that."

Patrek arched a tilted brow. "Commander, with all due respect, everyone on the ship heard it. We thought there was a problem in propulsion."

Rakon didn't know how close he was to the truth I hadn't yet shared with him. He'd likely get his chance to roar. I just hoped he had better control over his tiger than I did over mine. I supposed we'd find out if and when I ever got the chance to give him my mating bite.

He wrapped an arm around my shoulders, and we followed Patrek down the corridor toward the bridge. I don't know what I was expecting when he led me into a small closet. The space was tight with all three of us, and I fought off claustrophobia. I screeched in surprise when the closet shot upwards.

Hugging me tighter, he whispered, "Don't worry. It's a lift that takes us straight to the bridge. It just saves us climbing ladders."

"I think I would prefer the ladders." I turned my face into his chest. My tiger didn't like all these new things and made her displeasure evident. I pushed her down, telling her we were going to have to get used to things unless we wanted to go back to Earth. She grumbled again and only went quiet when I reminded her there were no fish on Earth.

I tested the constraints I'd put on her and found her sulking. She ignored my presence entirely. She could pout as long as she wanted if she'd only be quiet through this stupid meeting. I heard the shouting before the lift door opened.

"Spare us the melodrama, Father," Krenak snapped to an older man on the vidscreen. "You and Mother took great delight in telling everyone who would stand still about how she'd taken on two females for you. It's not as if War Mate Renata is any different. It's been years since any of us have seen a War Mate at all, so I'm not sure what you expected."

"Your mother didn't destroy anyone's hand."

"No, but one of those females lost an eye, didn't she? And Mother wasn't aggressive enough to be anyone's War Mate."

The man on the screen huffed irritably and didn't answer.

Another man spoke, his chilling words sending a roiling mixture of fear and anger through my belly. "The specimen has been proven to be dangerous. I think we should send it to sector four where it can be contained and studied." He sneered when he saw me.

I didn't understand the glint of avarice in his brown eyes or his immediate condemnation of me, but I knew when I was being sized up for something I wouldn't like. I had to get a handle on all these sectors too. What was special about them? I opened my mouth to speak, but Rakon beat me to it.

"Councilor Harkon, you must know that is quite impossible. If the Council is determined to keep her from Ximera, I will return her to Earth in accordance with our treaty. I would even go so far as to say that Earth would dissolve the treaty entirely and refuse us access to their females, especially after what happened with Renata and the other missing women."

Sweat popped on Harkon's brow, and he sputtered. "They can't—"

"I will also tender my resignation so I can stay with my mate. There are several unoccupied planets in the Camdar system, and I will make sure Markon and Denkar are aware of your unfortunate stroke of—"

Another man spoke, his voice low and gravelly, resonating

through the vidscreen. "Be silent, the both of you," he interrupted. "Harkon, your stupidity and willful ignorance of the terms of our treaty with Earth are beginning to irritate me, especially since you spent months cramming the damned thing down our throats."

He turned to face Rakon. "Speaking of which, Warlord. I received an interesting communication from Magistrate Smith on Earth. It seems you impressed upon him the importance of insisting that genetic mates be collected in person. We'll discuss it later. Rest assured your mate, along with any other shifter female, are welcome on any planet in our space."

I blinked at the male who had spoken. He was older even than Sendra had been. I'd never seen someone with so many years. His eyes were clouded with age, but must have been a stunning green in his youth. Wrinkles covered his face, deepening into crevasses when he smiled at me. Like Rakon, he wore a brand on his face, though it was faded and muddied with the lines of advanced age.

"Sit down, War Mate, and tell us what happened."

"Yes, sir." I perched on the edge of a chair, drawing a chuckle from Patrek that I didn't understand. Rakon looked amused but didn't say anything. "What do you want to know?"

"Tell us what happened from the time you left Earth with the Krenions."

"Yes, sir." I told the Ximeran Council my story, leaving out the part where I'd eaten the ship's crew. They didn't need to know. Horrified expressions on most of the males' faces made me relax. I hadn't thought they were responsible for my capture, but it was always good to get confirmation.

"You say they used a laser whip on your body?" the old male asked.

"Yes, sir."

"Quite impossible!" Harkon blustered. "Those things have been illegal for hundreds of cycles!"

Rakon arched an eyebrow and held up the black device that had caused me so much pain. He flicked the switch, turning on the lash. I flinched away and huddled back in my chair. I knew he wouldn't hurt me, but I couldn't stand to see it.

The smirk fell from his face when he looked at me, and he turned the horrible thing off. "As you can see, they do exist. I found this one on the transport we captured. Renata's wounds were consistent with what we know of its use."

"Thank you, Commander. War Mate, what happened with the female Merkella?"

"She pulled a knife on me, sir. I made her drop it."

"I see. Did she attack first?" The man stroked his whiskered jaw, the white hair rustling under his hand.

"Yes, sir. She cut my abdomen and told me she planned to kill me for my mate."

"I see. Do you have witnesses to this event?"

"Yes, sir. Everyone here was present in medical, plus a few others I don't see."

"Thank you." He looked over my head at Rakon. "Ensure Merkella doesn't leave confinement. If she requires treatment, I want two guards accompanying the medic."

"Sir?"

The old male's eyes softened as he looked at me. "What is it, War Mate?"

"What will happen to her?"

"She'll be tried and probably sent to sector nineteen for the remainder of her life. Attacking any female with the intent to kill is punishable by execution, but Merkella is female and fights between females for mates are encouraged."

I chewed on that for a moment. It seemed that female Ximerans had a great deal in common with my own animal nature. "Sir, I wish to speak."

"What is it, dear?"

"I would respectfully ask that you free Merkella when we reach Ximera."

"For what reason should we do this?" He leaned forward, his eyes seeming to see into my head even from the vidscreen.

I stood to face him eye to eye. "By your words, fights between females for mates are accepted in your culture, correct?"

"Yes. Are you making a point here?"

"Yes, sir. I do have a point. You wish to punish a female for engaging in a fight for dominance when such things are known and accepted. It is in direct contradiction of your laws."

He nodded. "You are quite correct, War Mate. In the normal course of things, we would have ignored your fight. However, we are now forced to take steps because of her threat to kill you. Even in the most vicious fights between potential War Mates, no female has ever died. I was fortunate enough to witness a few in my younger days." He stood and bowed to me, ignoring the gasps of surprise from both sides of the vidscreen.

"I applaud you, small human. You're logical, empathetic, and kind. You're a breath of fresh air to my old bones, and I look forward to meeting you in person." He straightened and winked at me. "Sadly, I doubt you'll have any challengers for your mate, but an old male can hope."

Clapping his hands together, he said, "This tribunal is over. Everyone out except Commander Rakon and the War Mate." When no one on his side of the screen moved, he scowled. "I said everyone, Councilors. Get off your fat asses and leave."

I let out a short bark of laughter. I really liked this old male. I had no doubt he would make a fearsome enemy. It was good that he seemed to like me. Patrek squeezed my shoulder in encouragement as he left.

"He won't hurt you. He's just old and a little set in his ways."

"I heard that! Get out before I reassign you to nineteen."

Patrek winced but left as he'd been ordered. I shook my head, unable to contain my giggles. When the old male winked, I laughed until tears streamed from my eyes. When I was able to breathe again, I said, "You're an old fraud, you know that? You won't send him to nineteen."

"Quiet, human! I have a reputation to uphold here!"

I laughed again. I really liked him. So did my tiger, and she rarely took to strangers. "I'm sorry, sir. What did you want to discuss with us?"

"Two things." He set his hard gaze on Rakon. "Commander, I ought to censure you for going above your station in dealing with the Earth Magistrate, but I won't because you were right. His communication demanded genetic proof of match before any human female is released to Ximera. It's going to be expensive and unwieldy, but we'll manage."

"Sir, may I say something?" I asked.

"Of course."

"Set up a regular shuttle schedule and take the females in groups. A few days one way or another isn't going to make much difference to anyone." I paused to observe his reaction. He looked at me expectantly as he waited for me to finish speaking.

"You should also have the Magistrate post a warning about the Krenion, and you could set up emergency shuttles if any female is in imminent danger of harm." I opened my mouth to speak, but shut it with a hard snap, unwilling to anger the old male.

"Go on, child. You obviously have something else to say."

"Negotiate with Earth to locate a permanent Ximeran base. It should be somewhere the women could wait in safety for their mates and would prevent another Krenion from sneaking through the cracks."

I grimaced. I didn't want to denigrate my home world, but I forced myself to continue. "Earth has no security. There aren't enough of us left to defend against anything, so if a large enough force of Krenions came, they could simply take what they wanted, and we couldn't stop them."

The old male peered over my head. His lips moved as if he was talking to himself, but he didn't say a word. I jumped when he slapped a hand down on the table. "Commander Rakon, your War Mate is a credit to you. Be sure that you're a credit to her as well. Do you think we'll encounter any difficulties, War Mate?"

"No, probably not. I doubt anyone would care, and it's not as if you'll be taking property owned by someone else. If you take over the exodus, I imagine there are many who would thank you."

"Very well. Consider it done. I'll begin the negotiations after we finish."

"Thank you. I also have other information I want to share, sir." I settled back into my chair. It was quite comfortable. I crossed my legs as I waited for the elder male's permission to speak.

"You look very good in the commander's chair, War Mate."

The tiger, possessive bitch that she was, wanted to claw the arms and leave her spoor so no one else sat in her chair. The human part of us had better sense. I had no idea how to fly a battle cruiser. However, it was Rakon's chair, and he was my mate, so...

Rakon grimaced as I popped a claw and dragged it down the arm of the chair, leaving a deep gouge. I straightened and refused to be embarrassed. "May I speak, sir?"

He chuckled and coughed to clear his throat. "Somehow, I don't think my words will stop you."

"With your permission, sir. The male who hurt me was Ximeran—"

"That is a very serious accusation," he interrupted. "Do you have proof?"

"Yes, sir. I bit off his leg before he escaped in a shuttle. He had long black hair and a white scar on his face."

"Did he mention a name or how he came to know about you?"

"No, sir."

"Norkad surely died when we blew up his ship, First Councilor. I don't see—"

"Did you see his body, Commander?"

Rakon looked down at his feet, his hands clenched with irritation. "Well, no."

"Then it is possible that he escaped. You know better than to think an explosion is proof of death."

Rakon scowled and opened his mouth to speak, but I raised my hand to interrupt him. "Sir, may I speculate?"

"Be my guest."

"Thank you. Humans were not aware of the existence of Krenions, and very few of us have seen a Ximeran in person. We'd barely made it to Mars with unmanned drones before the storms came. That means a Ximeran, or someone else not from Earth, knows about shifters. That person has taken or tried to take the only five to be found."

"Are you sure it couldn't have been a human?"

"No, sir. A human could very well be involved but would not have had the initial knowledge or the means to carry out a conspiracy of this scope. I have no idea what this Norkad person looks like, nor do I have any reason to lie. The male had a long white scar and is now missing his left leg. That is all either of us needs to know to track him down so I can eat him."

His eyes narrowed, and he looked down at a comm in his wrinkled hands. "One moment please, War Mate."

I nodded, and when the screen went dark, I looked questioningly at Rakon. A chime from the vidscreen drew my attention and I roared in anger. Instead of the old male, I faced my tormentor. The tiger forgot where we were and lunged for the screen, claws bared.

Our mate leaped in front of us. We skidded across the floor, desperate to avoid running him down. He dropped to his knees and wrapped his arms around our chest, stroking the sensitive skin between our ears. "Calm down, Renata. It's just a holo projection. It isn't him."

He said the words over and over. The soft sound of my mate's voice eventually penetrated our consciousness and we shifted, staring at the hateful face of the male who had hurt us. I tried very hard not to cry. He helped me dress, concealing me from the old Ximeran on the vidscreen.

The image disappeared and was replaced by a very stern-looking first councilor. "You fools didn't think to show her a picture." His words weren't a question. "The rumors of his demise are greatly exaggerated, it seems."

Rakon sat in the chair I'd occupied and settled me on his lap. I turned my face into his shoulder, knowing I shouldn't appear so weak in front of a potential enemy. I couldn't help it though. Just looking at an image of that vile male brought up memories best forgotten, and I shuddered at the phantom pain from that awful whip.

"Forgive me, First Councilor, but what the fuck was this little show supposed to prove?" His hand stroked my back, soothing me as he kissed my hair.

"You wanted proof that the male who took your War Mate was Norkad. You've got it, and so do I. I want him found and executed, and I want to see a carcass before your mate eats him."

Rakon stood, clutching me to his chest. "This conversation is over." Without another word, he strode from the bridge. The scent of his fury made my fangs itch.

CHAPTER

SIX

RAKON

I was silent as I carried Renata back to our quarters. She hadn't complained, but I heard her belly rumbling with hunger as I put her down. With any luck, the galley replicator had had enough time to produce more deer meat for her.

I was utterly furious at the first councilor's nasty trick. He hadn't even warned her what he intended to do. He'd wanted a natural reaction, but I wouldn't be able to speak to the old male with any degree of respect until I'd calmed both of us.

And part of my anger was directed at myself. I could have found a way to show her an image of Norkad myself without frightening her. I thanked all the old gods she hadn't shifted in front of the entire Council.

Despite her comforting presence, I couldn't help the jumble of thoughts racing through my head. I was damned proud of Renata. She'd been perfect. More perfect than I had any right to hope for, and I needed to find the words to tell her so without insulting her. I couldn't believe she hadn't growled at that imbecile Harkon. I'd wanted to tear his head off.

Yet I'd watched his face as she'd spoken of her ordeal. When the other members of the Council looked horrified, he'd appeared bored. He'd been the original drafter of the treaty between Earth and Ximera and had shouted from the rooftops about its benefit to our people. Yet now, he blatantly ignored the terms he'd written, denigrating the very females he'd wanted introduced into Ximeran society. By his actions, he'd put Renata at risk when he'd sent me into seventeen on a fruitless mission.

I also had to consider her speculation. It made me ill to think that one of my own people would stoop so low as to do business with a Krenion, but her words made too much sense. I also had to remember that some of the bodies we'd found on that transport had been Ximeran. I shook away the thoughts. Council members were beyond reproach. They were thought to be the wisest and most honest of us. Perhaps I was looking for conspiracies that weren't there.

"Did I do something wrong, Rakon? I didn't mean to shift like that, and I'm sorry if it caused trouble."

Her voice was too small and nervous, and I kicked myself for not giving her the encouragement and praise she was due. I forced out a laugh and picked her up off her feet. She squealed when I swung her in a circle. Kissing her forehead, and then her delicious lips because I couldn't not kiss her, I said, "You are going to be an amazing War Mate, Renata. I can't believe how calm and collected you were. You are so intelligent, and your conclusions were brilliant!"

I scowled and pointed at my own chest. "Whereas your illustrious mate wanted to rip Harkon's head right off his shoulders and sh..." I stopped. That wasn't an appropriate thing to say to one's mate, even if she was a War Mate. "Anyway, you were magnificent. I can't believe how you charmed the first councilor. He hates everyone, and he scares the piss out of me."

"I thought I would like him, but—"

"I'm not particularly happy with him at the moment either, but I understand his reasoning. He wanted to see your reaction when you saw Norkad."

She nodded against my chest. "I get it, but that doesn't mean I like it."

Pressing my palm against the control panel outside our quarters, I said, "We also need to get your palm entered into the computer so you can move freely about the ship. I meant to do it earlier."

"It's okay. We've had a busy morning. Can we do it after we eat?"

"Of course. I also want to see if we can get the computer to accept your paw. That way, your tiger will be able to negotiate the ship too."

I had no idea what I said, but I suddenly had an armful of warm woman who seemed intent on devouring my lips. Whatever it was, I'd have to remember it. The door opened, and she pushed me inside, never ceasing her delicious kisses. I hissed as the sharp point of one of her upper canines pricked my lip.

She lapped at the blood and made that low rumbling I'd learned meant she was pleased by something. The sound made me so damned hard it felt like all the blood in my body rushed to my cock. I swung her into my arms and carried her to the couch, then sat, arranging her so she straddled my lap.

Her busy hands stroked my chest as she licked at my lower lip, her vibrating noise of pleasure sinking deep into my skin. I buried my hands in her hair, tilting her head for better access to her luscious mouth.

My hands loosened their grip on her hair as she rubbed her core against my cock, and I let my head fall backward in pleasure as she ground herself against me. To my surprise, she dropped to her knees between my thighs. With a careful claw, she shredded my uniform trousers, baring my cock.

When I tried to push her away, claws erupted from her fingertips, and she grasped my hands to hold me still as she sucked the head of my cock into her sweet mouth.

"Fuck!"

The word was torn from my mouth as she swallowed me, my cock hitting the back of her throat. She coughed once, then resumed the rumbling vocalization, sending electric pleasure through my body. Stars! The vibrations from her throat made me helpless to her aggressive sucking of my flesh.

~

RENATA

Rakon tasted so damned good. His blood was the second-best thing I'd ever tasted. It was second only to the taste of the fluid leaking from the tip of his cock. The mating gland behind my upper canines spilled its fluid into my mouth, making me swallow around his turgid flesh.

We wanted to bite so badly, but not in this spot. We wanted to leave a mating scar everyone would see, and the thought of someone else seeing Rakon's beautiful cock made us growl. He hissed at the additional vibration, his cock swelling in my mouth. My tiger had never been so close to the surface without shifting. Rakon's blood enticed her into playing, though she seemed content to let me keep control. I thanked her with a whispered purr. Growing fur right now would have been... unfortunate.

He stopped struggling, his hands lax in my grip as I sucked him. Releasing one of his wrists, I brought my hand between his legs to fondle his balls. His delicious scent enveloped me, sending my tiger into raptures as she rolled in pleasure. I could do this all day.

"Renata, please. I'm going to..."

Yes, please. I moved my hand deeper between his legs, searching out the sensitive spot between his ass and balls. Rubbing firmly, I took him as deeply as I could and purred around his flesh. He smelled so damned good; his arousal made my pussy wet with want.

Virile male and something spicy filled my nose, making us want to roll in the scent until it covered us.

The feel of his hard flesh swelling in my mouth was indescribably good. I wanted more. I wanted to suck his cock forever. I tightened my hand around the base of his cock, careful to keep my claws sheathed. He cried out, sinking his hands into my hair as he thrust into my mouth.

Growling, he stood, looming over me as he tugged my hair to make me meet his eyes. His pupils dilated with pleasure as he bared his teeth. The sight made me drip for him, and my pussy slicked as it readied itself for mating. Still holding the base of his cock, I fondled his heavy sac with my free hand. I loved the weight and scent of him, adored the silky-soft hair covering his balls.

My hands were wet with the sweetness leaking from his cock as well as from the fluid leaking from my mating gland. Dragging a finger through the delectable juice, I rubbed his tight rosebud, easing a finger inside as I searched for the place that would give him incredible pleasure if he was similar in physiology to a human. To my delight, I found it, and rubbed firmly as I swallowed his delicious cock.

With a shout, he erupted, spilling his cum into my mouth. It mixed with the liquid from my mating gland, creating a sweet, sticky mixture that made me want more. I wasn't exactly inexperienced, but I'd never tasted anything so delicious. There was the bit of male salt I was used to, but it was rich and earthy. I sucked every drop I could from his body until he twitched and hissed as I lapped at the sensitive head of his cock.

With a groan of repletion, he pulled me into his lap and kissed me. I shared the taste of my delicious treat with him, and he growled in approval as he wrapped his arms around me. Pulling back, he cupped my face in his hands and asked, "What was that for?"

"You offered to put our paw into your computer. That's the nicest thing anyone has ever done for me. I can't tell you what it means to know that you accept my tiger."

His eyes half closed in pleasure, Rakon stroked my face. "Did you worry I wouldn't?" he asked.

I looked away, unwilling to meet his gaze when I replied. "Yes. There are a few things you don't know, and we need to talk."

~

RAKON

No male in the universe ever wanted to hear those words. They were the kiss of death, and every male I knew would chew off his own arm to avoid them. Yet Renata didn't engage in useless conversation about her feelings. Rather, I'd been the one to force her into sharing when I'd felt she'd been hiding something. Whatever she had to say was critical and affected both of us.

Part of me wondered if she'd given me such amazing oral sex to soften me up for whatever she had to say, but she'd enjoyed herself too much. Truthfully, I didn't think she was that devious. Merkella had been one of those females who would exchange sex for favors. I knew the difference between manipulation and pleasure.

"All right. Let me get our lunch ordered. We can eat while we talk." I held her hand as I put the call in to the galley. They'd managed to produce fifty kilos of the meat she'd liked. I hoped it would be enough for her. Her eyes widened at the amount, and I wondered if she'd ever been able to eat her fill.

"I'm going to take a quick shower while we wait. Is that okay?"

"Of course. We'll see about getting you some more clothes after our talk."

"Thanks." Without another word, she walked into the lavatory, and I heard the sonic shower kick on. I couldn't wait to get her home. I had a shower with real water and a soaking tub big enough for two—or for her tiger. She would love the water, but I doubted her tiger would be impressed at the size. She probably wouldn't be able to turn around easily. I lived close enough to the ocean that we could go any time, and I knew that would please her.

I couldn't wait to see how she handled the larger fish present in our oceans. Some of them were as big as her tiger.

"What's so funny?" She was dressed in her pants from before but had changed into one of my shirts. I loved seeing her in my clothes. My brush was in her hand, and she struggled to drag it through the tangled mass of gold-and-black streaks.

"Here, let me do that." I had her sit on the floor between my knees as I worked the brush through her luxuriant mane. Compared to her tiger's rough fur, her human hair was like the finest *ganko* threads. The fabric woven from the silk of the *ganko* spider was so rare it was reserved only for special occasions. We used it for burials and weddings, and I'd only ever touched my mother's gown from her joining to my father. I hoped Renata would consent to wear that dress at our joining.

"You didn't tell me why you were laughing when I came out of the lavatory. Do I look that weird in your shirt?"

"You look beautiful in my shirt. If we didn't have lunch coming, I'd insist you wear nothing else."

She blushed and lowered her head. I didn't think anyone had given her compliments before, but she had to know how beautiful she was—in both her forms. "I was laughing because I thought about you in the ocean near our home. There are fish as big as your tiger, and I was picturing you wrestling with one."

"Are they good to eat?"

"Yes. Fishermen catch them all the time. They're numerous and a favored food of many Ximerans."

"Then I will catch one for you. What are they called?"

My little War Mate was stalling. She wanted to tell me something very badly but didn't want to start the conversation. I pulled her to my lap. "You said we had to talk. Why don't you tell me what you need to say?"

The comm unit sounded, announcing our lunch. "Saved by the

bell, it seems." I stood and put her in the chair, pointing a finger at her. "Stay right there while I get our food."

She snapped at my finger but hadn't been serious. I still had it attached to my hand, after all. I counted that a win. The steward rolled in a cart, piled with steaming dishes. "Sir, the cook thought the War Mate might enjoy trying some Ximeran food. He doesn't think..." The steward shut his mouth. "I'm sorry, sir. You'll have to take it up with him."

"It's fine. Tell him I'll have the War Mate discuss her diet with him at her convenience."

"Yes, Commander. I'll give him the message."

I pushed the cart toward the table. "I'm sorry. I'd planned on giving you more meat, but my cook had other ideas."

"It's okay. I can't eat chunks of raw meat in my human form, and everything smells delicious." She seated herself across from me and waited expectantly while I filled her plate. After I'd set her food in front of her, she picked up her fork and took a bite of steamed *mara*. Her eyes flew open, and she let them close as she chewed. Her sensual moan of bliss made my cock hard enough to hammer metal pins into deck plate.

When she finished chewing, she said, "You're right. I was stalling." Putting her fork down, she stared at me. "I have to tell you about myself. Well, I suppose about all shifters. We come in two types."

She took another huge mouthful and swallowed it. I don't think she tasted the food at all. "All right. What are the two types?"

"We're either born, like me, or we're bitten."

"I don't understand what that means. I understand born, but what does bitten mean?"

"This is so hard." She took another bite of her food, and I wanted to steal the plate away and make her speak. "I'm a born tiger. My father was born, but my mother was bitten. She'd been human before that."

"Continue, please." I had no idea where she was going with her thoughts, but I did have some suspicions and they made my belly clench.

"Nobody ever told me how to do this," she muttered around another bite of food. "When my father met my mother, he knew they were genetic mates. He convinced her to accept a mating bite, which changed her into a bitten tiger."

"What stops you from biting several people to increase your genetic diversity?"

"We can only bite one person, and a bitten shifter can never administer a mating bite."

"Why not? You should have been biting humans all over Earth!"

"It doesn't work that way." She sipped from her water glass and cleared her throat. "Born shifters have a gland in their mouths, behind the upper canine teeth. When we administer our mating bite, we empty the contents of that gland into our chosen mate, and the organ reabsorbs into our bodies. Bitten shifters never get that extra organ, and we can only do it once."

"I see. Aside from that gland, what are the differences between bitten and born tigers?"

"They're indistinguishable, especially after a born shifter has bitten a mate."

I thought I knew where this line of conversation was headed, and I didn't know what to think. It was too much, too fast. "What does that mean for me?"

She lowered her head until I couldn't see her face. "It means that if we mate, I will bite you. I won't be able to help myself. And then you will shift."

RENATA

I flinched when the door shut behind him. If it was an Earth door with hinges and a latch, it would have slammed.

I should have known Rakon wouldn't accept me. I was too alien. Too violent and aggressive. Too... different. My tiger paced irritably, calling me names she shouldn't have known. She'd advised that we bite first and answer questions later. I'd ignored her. No shifter wanted an unwilling mate. Despite our animals, we kept just enough humanity to give our mates the choice. My mother hadn't known anything about born shifters, but she'd impressed that upon me at a very early age. Sendra had only needed to reinforce the lesson as she explained how it would work.

Picking up my fork, I ate mechanically. The food was delicious, and I wanted at least one good meal before Rakon returned me to Earth. Maybe I would find another mate. I also resolved to tell the old male from Rakon's council about what happened with shifters, despite my reluctance to speak with him. Rakon had walked into the situation blind. The logical part of me knew that and didn't mind his hasty exit from my presence. My tiger and my emotions were another matter.

I should have known better than to hope. As Sendra would have said, "Do not pass Go, do not collect two hundred dollars." I had no idea what Go was, but the last part referred to money. She'd had so many of those little sayings that hadn't made sense. I wondered if I should keep my genetics in the Ximeran database but decided against it. We'd already found our mate and been rejected.

My tiger yowled in anger, but I knew it was for the best. I would spend my time with the Magistrate and help locate other shifters. Finding them homes in a clean environment would ease the ache in my chest. Maybe.

Maybe in a few dozen years, this would be a bittersweet memory. I ate everything on the table. Good food would be a bittersweet memory faster than Rakon.

The vidscreen on the wall chimed, and I looked up into kind green eyes. The first councilor grinned at me, and I burst into tears.

"No, child! Don't cry. You're breaking this old male's heart in half. Why are you crying? I'm so sorry I hurt you when I showed you that picture. You must stop now that I've apologized!"

I had to chuckle through my tears, but they didn't stop streaming down my face. "No. I can't. He won't let me…" My voice dissolved into sobs again, and I wanted to kick myself. When had I started acting like a character from one of Sendra's stupid romance novels?

"Get me a shuttle right now. I need to be on Rakon's ship yesterday." I heard his voice over the vidscreen but ignored it.

"Renata, look at me and take a deep breath."

I looked up into his wise old eyes and inhaled. The breath calmed me and stopped the hitching in my chest. "I'm sorry, sir."

"Don't be. Tell me what happened."

I don't think I explained everything as clearly as I'd hoped, but he nodded in understanding when I'd finished. My throat hurt, and I had a headache. The tiger sulked in a corner of my head, soothed by the old male's presence, but still pissed at me.

I lowered my eyes from his piercing stare.

"Do you mean to tell me that little whelp refused your bite? Female, if I were ten years younger, I'd push him out of the way of your teeth."

I giggled and wiped my eyes on the sleeve of my—no, Rakon's shirt. It would serve him right if I ruined it with my snot.

"You don't have to laugh. It's probably more like fifty years."

I sniffed and looked up. He reminded me so much of Sendra and not because of their age. He was like her in that he didn't mince words. He didn't say things he didn't mean. I fell a little in love with him for that.

"What should I do, sir?"

"First, don't call me sir. It makes me feel ancient and the idiots on the Council call me sir. Call me Fengar."

"Thanks. You can call me Renata, even though I know it's only for mates. It's not like anyone else will care."

"Don't sell the whelp short. You've given him a surprise none of us saw coming. Rest assured that every single Ximeran male who seeks a shifter mate will be aware of what will be required of them."

"Sir, your shuttle is ready."

"Thank you." He turned back to me and said, "I'll be there tomorrow morning. Don't do anything rash until I get there."

"Rash?"

"Yes. Don't kill him. Don't steal a shuttle to make your way back to Earth. Don't do anything you might regret." He stroked his bristly jaw. "In fact, if you can find a bolt-hole, use it."

"Yes, sir."

RAKON

I spent time walking through Renata's sim and thinking. I probably shouldn't have left her alone, but her news overwhelmed me. The logical part of me recoiled in horror at the idea of turning into an animal, yet the inner, feral bit of me that made me a Warlord was excited. What must it be like to share brain space with a wild creature?

I squatted next to the lake where she'd swum, remembering how she'd leaped into the water. How far had she jumped? It was certainly farther than I could. I pressed my hand into her paw print. No one had used the sim since her visit yesterday. It was the size of the plate I'd used to serve her lunch and set knuckle deep into the loose sand.

She was massive; at least three hundred kilos or a little more, judging by the depth of the print. How did she fit that huge creature into her tiny body? I would admit to some curiosity, but I didn't know if it was enough to allow the bite that would change my life. Would I be content in my battle cruiser?

I sat and thought for a long time, long enough to hear the click and whir of lights dimming into simulated dusk over Renata's lake.

When I stood, my bones ached from my position. I cracked my neck and made my way back toward the entrance to the holo.

I wasn't sure if I was ready to give up my life in the stars for a life of fur and claw, but I knew I wasn't ready to give up Renata.

When I exited the holo, three of my own males were waiting for me, blasters pointed at my chest. One smirked, but wiped the expression from his face as Patrek approached.

"Would someone care to tell me why my crew is committing mutiny?"

"We are not mutinying. We are ordered by First Councilor Fengar to hold you in custody until he arrives in the morning."

"On what charge?"

Patrek pulled a tablet from his pocket and read from it. "His direct message to me was, 'Lock that idiotic whelp up until I have time to deal with his stupidity.' Do you wish to refute the charges, Commander?"

"What happened?"

"Apparently, he signaled the vid in your quarters, and Renata started to cry."

I winced, and a few of the males gave me sympathetic looks before turning their faces back to Patrek. "No, I do not refute the charges."

"Wise choice, sir."

I followed him down into the lower decks to my own containment area. Merkella huddled in a cell in the corner and didn't acknowledge our presence. Someone must have told her that her ploy hadn't worked.

Surprisingly, Patrek slipped into my cell before the guards closed the energy field. He lowered himself to the narrow cot in the corner and leaned his weight back on his palms. "Want to talk about it?"

"Not really." I sighed and sat next to him. "It's going to come out soon enough, I expect. Renata shared with me what happens when shifters choose a mate, and the news was... unexpected."

He lifted his shoulders in a nonchalant shrug. "I'm not sure what you expected, sir. How did you think the shifters reproduce?"

"I hadn't thought about it."

Scowling, he glared at me, his face tight with annoyance. "What's the problem? You let your gorgeous War Mate sink those pretty teeth into you and you get to go furry. Several enterprising souls have already been to see me, hoping to snag a shifter mate for their own."

"I beg your pardon?" What sort of males did I have on my ship that they would seek out a shifter's life? "How did you know?"

"The first councilor. He wants the news spread far and wide to prevent your unfortunate reaction." He chuckled softly. "He called it an appalling lack of good sense."

"Ouch."

"He spread the news on Ximera, and the whole planet is shut down."

My mouth fell open in shock. "What for?"

"They're all waiting for a transport to Earth. Some benighted soul decided it was better to search the planet inch by inch for shifters than to wait for the females to come forward. They can't all go, of course. The first councilor ordered a lottery."

"I can't even imagine that of our people. It seems insane that so many would choose to embrace an animal."

He leaned forward, resting his elbows on his knees. "Can't you? Think about it. War Mate Renata singlehandedly wiped out an entire crew on a large transport and managed to take a chunk from Norkad." He stroked his chin and grinned. "Or would that be single-pawedly? I don't think she used her hands."

"I simply can't believe a Ximeran would—"

"You're not helping your case, Commander," he warned. "I've already done the analysis on the remains. The limb definitely came from a Ximeran. And given what the first councilor told me about War Mate Renata's reaction to Norkad's image, I'm willing to believe the renegade has returned."

"But—"

He continued speaking and didn't allow me a word. "And after she killed the entire crew, she ate them. Aside from the cuts from the laser whip and the blaster shot to her hip, which I might add didn't seem to affect her enough to slow her down, she exited that transport without injury. How many males would we have lost in such a battle?"

Standing, he added, "Think about it. What would you give for such power?" He paused and looked away. "I plan to tender my resignation when we reach Ximera, Commander."

I stood and raised my hands. I didn't want to lose my science officer and friend. "What? Why?"

He grinned crookedly. "I looked up wolves in the database. If they're not extinct, I'm going to find her."

"Her, who?"

He deactivated the energy field long enough to exit and reset it to close me in. "My future mate and the mother of my cubs. Renata is a beautiful animal, but I've never seen such intelligence in the eyes of a beast as I did in those wolves. Besides, they're small enough I won't have to reinforce the furniture."

Whistling softly, he left me alone. I sighed and walked across my cell to the small replicator. It was only programmed to provide a few meal choices and water. I'd missed both lunch and the evening meal, and my body was beginning to complain. I hoped that Renata was able to eat. She needed everything I could give her.

Would it be so bad to share my mind with a tiger? Obviously, I was in the minority on this decision. I couldn't believe my overzealously pedantic science officer was going off into the desolation of Earth to search out a wolf. I didn't even know what a wolf was.

I had to give Renata my admiration once again. She'd given me the information and a choice when she could have simply administered her bite and let me deal with the consequences. She already had my respect, but I felt a little bit of something else creep into the seething mess of my thoughts.

"She's a mutant, you know." Merkella's voice echoed in the small containment facility, and I tried to ignore her. "Those animals are going to ruin our bloodlines."

"We have no bloodlines, former Medic. You know perfectly well we're dying out."

"Harkon says…" She went quiet, and I wished I could wrap my hands around her neck and force her to speak. The councilor had come up in conversation once too many times for my liking.

"What did Councilor Harkon say?"

"Never mind." She chuckled softly. "I thought we would mate."

"That would never have happened." The words came without thought. Merkella was beautiful and an entertaining bed partner, but cold and harsh. She didn't have enough strength to become a War Mate, relying instead on lies and subterfuge to gain advantage. I heard her sigh, but I wouldn't take the words back. She didn't deserve my consideration after her actions.

"What did Harkon say?" I asked again.

"It isn't important." She laughed softly. "You'll find out sooner or later, anyway."

Despite further efforts, she refused to speak again.

CHAPTER
SEVEN

RENATA

"I don't want to play that game." I listened to the whine in my voice. I was acting like a spoiled brat, but I couldn't help myself. It felt good to wallow in self-pity for an evening. To his credit, my guest didn't say anything about my attitude and put away the card game he'd tried to teach me.

Patrek clicked the remote for the vidscreen, bringing up some old Earth show I didn't recognize. Whatever electricity we'd managed to generate on Earth had gone toward heating and boiling water. There hadn't been any to spare for watching vids.

The vid was colorless. Sendra had a name for it, but I couldn't remember what she'd called it. The actors in the vid were rendered in shades of gray and black. A somewhat shrill woman yelled to a dark-haired male called Ricky. I heard laughter in the background, so I could only assume the ancient humans had found the couple's antics amusing. I didn't see the point.

"You don't like it?" Patrek asked.

"I don't understand it. I have no frame of reference."

"A pity. This is one of the commander's favorites." He thumbed through the selections, scrolling almost too fast for me to read.

"Wait! I want that one."

"Midsummer Night's Dream?"

"Yes!" I bounced excitedly in my chair. Sendra had read that one to me and I loved it. I couldn't wait to see it on the vid.

"All right, War Mate, but if we're going to watch a vid of this length, we're going to do it right."

"What does that mean?"

"Popcorn, chocolate, and carbonated drinks with lots of sugar. That's what ancient humans ate when they watched vids."

"I don't know what those things are."

"Not to worry. I promise you'll love it all." He tapped on his comm to place the order.

I was already engrossed in the action on the vidscreen and missed the hail from the door. But then I smelled the most delicious odor. It was fat and salt carried by something sweet, and my mouth watered instantly.

Patrek set a huge bowl of fluffy white things between us on the couch. Whatever it was, it was the source of that divine scent. I looked around for a utensil until I noticed him use his hand to scoop up a small pile of the white objects. I did the same.

I nearly died of pleasure at the first taste of the greasy salty goodness that is popcorn. The tiger even crawled out from her snit at the first taste and smacked her lips for more before remembering she was supposed to be mad at me.

Patrek jerked his hand away from the bowl when I growled and snapped. I covered my hot face in mortification. "I am so sorry!"

"It's fine, War Mate. I'll order more." He scowled at me as he typed in his request. "But you have to share the chocolate. Don't make me sorry for letting you have some of it."

I pulled the bowl into my lap, crouching over it protectively. Maybe someday my food aggression would go away. It was illogical and stupid, but I couldn't help it. "I really am sorry, Patrek. I don't know why I still do that."

"You're a tiger. I've been researching your animal, and it's your nature to guard food for your cubs. You might never get over it, and it will probably get worse when you have young ones."

"How do you know all this?"

"We downloaded your Library of Congress. I doubt it's the sum of human knowledge, but there is quite a lot of information to be had there. Other teams are working on the repositories from other countries, but I was on the team for the former United States. Anyway, there's all sorts of information about large predators."

"Why were you researching me?" I ate another few pieces of popcorn as he rose to answer the door for the second bowl.

He settled back on the couch. "Several reasons. I wanted to learn about you so I could help you acclimate to your new surroundings. Did you know that tigers were among the rarest of the apex predators on your world?"

"Yes, my mother told me I was the last, and my friend Sendra said we'd always been uncommon even before the storms. She was an old jackal, and very wise."

"Well, my theory is that if you managed to survive, there will definitely be others. I plan to seek out the wolves and bring them back to Ximera."

"There aren't any. They're extinct."

He smirked and tapped my nose. "I think you're wrong. I think they're hiding just like you did. And I know where I might find them." He paused the vid and pulled up a map.

I'd seen maps of the old United States, and I knew what I was looking at. He pointed to an area several hundred miles west of my home territory in Georgia. "I think they'll be in this place called Wyoming. Surface scans show life there, and the area seems to be less affected by the storms, possibly due to the altitude. Wolves are also a quarter of your size. They can survive on less food and tend to live in packs so they would be hunting cooperatively."

He snapped the map away, returning the play to the vidscreen. "I suppose it's possible they've moved. After all, you were found halfway across the planet from your place of origin near the Arctic circle. I'll try Alaska if I don't have any luck in Wyoming. Now watch your show, and I'll give you chocolate later."

I shook my head and settled back with my popcorn. He was a lot smarter than me and knew where to find information I wouldn't even know I wanted. If he said there might be wolves out there, I believed him. And I believed he would find them.

The vid was over too soon, but I was exhausted from my day and yawned as Patrek cleaned up our food. I'd loved the chocolate, but it was almost too sweet. He said it was because I'd never had much sugar. The drinks were too sticky and made my teeth hurt.

With a stomach full of popcorn, I escorted him to the door. "Thanks for sitting with me. I was glad to not be left alone tonight." I chewed my lip for a moment, relishing the last of the salt from the popcorn. "Do you know where Rakon went?"

"He's in a cell in confinement by order of the first councilor. You don't have to worry he'll bother you tonight."

"But... Why?"

"Because he made you cry, and the first councilor didn't like it." He dropped a chaste kiss on my forehead. "Get some sleep, War Mate."

I caught his arm before he left. "Wait! Can you help me put my hand into your computer so I can get around the ship? Rakon said he would, but we never got to do it."

He stared at me pensively, and I had to wonder what he was thinking. "No, not tonight. We'll do it first thing in the morning."

"Why? It keeps getting shuffled off to the side, and I don't want to be trapped here."

Chucking me under my chin, he said, "I'll make a deal with you. I'll set access for this door and the door to the galley. I want you and Commander Rakon to have a night to think and I suspect you're going to run down to confinement the first chance you get."

"And the holo." I didn't disagree with him.

He laughed. "And the holo. Give me your hand."

I nodded as he laid my palm against the panel by the door. He was probably right about what I would do. But he was also right when he said I should give us both a chance to cool off and think.

The panel beeped and a computerized voice said, "Access for War Mate Renata is accepted." I had no plans to venture out, but it was a relief to be able to leave if I wished. The tiger huffed out a pleased growl, adding her approval of my actions.

The door slid closed, leaving me alone. Despite my peace offering of popcorn and the freedom to leave Rakon's quarters, my tiger was still pissed. I'd often wondered what it would be like to live without her scathing commentary. Now that I knew, I didn't like it.

After washing up, I crawled into Rakon's bed, clutching his pillow to my face. I inhaled his scent into my lungs. I didn't need to memorize the odor; it was already embedded in my body.

The tiger turned her back to me, curling up in a furry heap in the recesses of my mind. "I'm sorry," I offered. "I know you don't under-stand, but I had to give him a choice. Neither of us wants a mate that hates us."

Her ear twitched, but she didn't respond so I tried again. "He's a proud, strong male. If we had lied, he would have been hurt and very angry."

I got another ear twitch and a ruffling of fur. *So?*

"He might have refused us cubs."

He wouldn't dare.

"Maybe. I wasn't willing to take the risk. Think about how we felt when we were taken captive. It would have been the same for him."

I want him to be tiger. You will fix this.

"I do too." She didn't answer. Instead, she sent me images of the holo and I decided to make another peace offering. It wouldn't be the first time we'd slept in fur. After I dressed, I found the galley. A sleepy steward gave me a container of meat, telling me it would keep my breakfast fresh until I wanted it. I found my way to the place we would den for the night.

~

RAKON

I roused blearily to the sound of metal banging on the sides of my cell. "Wake up, boy. You and I are going to have a talk."

My head fell back to the thin pillow. I'd been having a wonderful dream about running through a cold forest, soft leaf litter under my paws as I chased my striped mate. She would lift her tail and I'd mount her, gripping her neck in a mating bite... The dream changed, and suddenly I was fucking her in the massive bed in my house on Ximera 8. Though we wore skin instead of fur, I claimed her from behind. Her hands were bound, stretched out in front of her, and her ass was pink from a thorough spanking.

My rational mind might have some questions about my decision, but my body and heart were on board with going furry. I'd spent most of the uncomfortable night mulling it over. While tremendously enjoyable, the erotic dreams left me frustrated and wanting.

Rubbing my eyes, I sat up. "Do come in, First Councilor. I'm afraid I can't offer you tea."

"Don't be snide. You're an idiot, and I should lock you in nineteen until you grow a damned spine."

"Yes, sir."

The guard released the force field, and to my surprise, left it off as the aged male stomped into my cell. He gestured imperiously, and I moved over to allow him to sit on the narrow cot.

"You made her cry. War Mates don't cry. They send whatever made them unhappy to medical in pieces."

"Renata is a kind and generous person!" I protested. "She would do no such thing!" I winced as I looked over at Merkella's cell. Our cells were at opposite sides and I couldn't see her. "Well, not without reason, anyway." When he didn't reply, I said, "And you have no right to disparage her."

The first councilor winked, and a smile played about his lips under his thick beard. "That's my boy."

Cagey old male. He'd baited me. I sighed and looked away, knowing I would lose at whatever game he was playing.

"As Science Officer Patrek has probably already told you, we've shared the unique needs of the shifters with the rest of the population."

I had a sudden thought that made my belly clench. "Did you get word to Dakar and Markon? They're looking for their mates."

"Yes. Dakar has a lead on Chen Daiyu's location. With luck, he'll bring her home soon."

"What about Markon? He mentioned chasing down a lead on that pirate blowing up sector eight, but he doesn't seem to care about Soledad."

His lips set into a firm line. "You know more than I do, then. The communication to Warlord Markon was received and read, but he didn't reply. I'm going to have to yank a knot in that boy's tail one of these days."

I was glad to hear someone was in worse trouble than I was, but I was worried as well. Despite his irascible nature, it was unlike Markon to ignore communications. Granted, his replies were terse to the point of rudeness, but he always responded. "I think more crews would be helpful. Markon is..." I trailed off, unwilling to say the word.

"Markon is unstable and untrustworthy. If I had a choice in the matter, I'd see that the Martinez female got another mate. She's too valuable and important to risk on a male who should have been forcibly retired years ago."

I winced at the harsh description, but I wasn't about to argue. It was true. If Markon couldn't pull himself together in time to satisfy the first councilor, he'd likely be declared rogue.

"Now that we've gotten the unimportant things out of the way, what have you decided?"

Standing, I stretched, relishing the creak of muscle and bone as my back cracked. "I'm going to find my War Mate and get furry, sir."

He clapped his hands together as an expression of glee crossed his face. "I can't wait to see it!"

"No. Mine." The low growl vibrating my throat surprised us both. I cleared my throat. "I beg your pardon, sir."

He cackled and slapped my back. "Sounds like you're already halfway there. Your mate is in the holo. I want this done before the evening meal."

I didn't answer. I left him alone in the cell as I raced toward my mate. There was going to be biting, and I wasn't taking no for an answer.

The holo door opened soundlessly, letting me into Renata's sim. It was still frigid, but the morning sun sparkled off the dew-covered plants. Patrek had outdone himself on this environment. If I hadn't known better, I'd swear I was in an alpine meadow.

My steps took me toward the lake, following her spoor. A broken stasis container rested under a bush, scraps of raw meat evidence of her morning meal, but another rested next to it. Normally, those containers were impervious to zero gravity and small strikes by space debris, but obviously didn't stand up to Renata's claws and teeth. I grinned and filed that useful tidbit away for further consideration.

A twig snapped and I froze, questioning my life choices. I'd blithely walked into a sim, knowing I was approaching a tiger with an undetermined mood. When faced with an angry predator, the best offense is to run like hell, or stand as still as possible and forget to breathe until the danger passed. Despite my prehistoric brain stem's admonishments, I planted my feet and waited.

She would either kill me or not, but I would not run from my own mate.

Renata approached me on dirty bare feet. She was dressed in my shirt and nothing else, just like I'd imagined her the day before. I'd wondered if she tolerated the cold in her human form, and she'd given me the answer without words. I wondered if she knew her own physical limitations.

"You spoiled our chase. So did Fengar. He said he was too old to run, but he scratched our ears and between our shoulder blades where we can't reach."

"I'm sorry. And I'm sorry for making you cry. I shouldn't have left you like that."

She sat down next to my feet, her knees drawn up to her chest. I scooted behind her and pulled her into my arms, cradling her thin body against me. She probably wasn't interested in getting comfort from me, but I was going to offer it whether she liked it or not.

And just when had she gotten to be on a first-name basis with the first councilor? I wasn't even sure his mate had called him by his given name.

"I'm sorry I didn't tell you sooner. I tried to say something a few times, but something always seemed to distract us," she said.

"When is a good time to tell someone that they're going to grow claws and four feet?"

She laughed and leaned her head back against my chest. "Have you decided when you're going to take me back to Earth?"

"You're not going back to Earth. At least, not without me. And definitely not before you've given me the bite you owe me."

She turned to face me, and her joyful smile stole my wind. Putting her small hands on my cheeks, she lifted her lips to mine in a sweet, too damned short kiss. I tried to pull her back for more, but she darted away, laughing.

Groaning in disappointment, I stood and adjusted my cock in my uniform pants.

"Why can't we get to the biting?"

She stayed a careful distance away, but her hands clenched as black claws popped from her fingers. Stripes dusted her face before fading. "It's all I can do to hold back, but we can't. We need to talk."

"No more talking. I always mess up when we talk. More kissing. And biting. And then I can get furry, and we can swim." I stalked toward her, but she danced out of my reach.

"You don't mess up when we talk. I'm the one who messes up. Besides, we need to talk to the Krenion and reach Ximera before I give you my bite." She darted away, avoiding my grasp.

"Someone else can do it." My mate was stalling again.

"No! I want to look in his face when he tells us why the Ximeran hired him to take me. And I want to share my bite when we're on Ximera and completely safe."

"That's not the only reason. Tell me."

She settled to the ground and leaned back against a tree, her legs crossed in front of her. "Think about it, love—"

"What?" My voice was sharp with disappointment, but I adored hearing her call me "love." I wondered if it was intentional and prayed to all the old gods she meant it.

"I don't know how long it will be before your tiger comes out to play. It's different for every species, but when he comes, I don't know how much of your rational mind will be there for those first few days." She choked out a short laugh. "This is very hard for me. My tiger is only interested in three things right now. She only wants to feed, fight, and fuck, in that order."

She patted the ground next to her, and I sank down beside her. "I was thirteen the first time I shifted, and my mother locked me in a cage in our basement to keep me hidden and safe. It drove my tiger insane, and it was almost a month before my mother could reach me through her rage. If I bite you now, on this ship, you might do the same thing."

I stared at her, horrified. "How could your mother do such a thing?"

"She didn't have a choice. There were too many people and not enough space to allow us to run and work through things on our own. It's likely we'd have been shot or hurt someone. She said she was feral for about a week after my father's bite, but he was able to take her somewhere she and her tiger could run and hunt."

"What does that mean for me?" I tried not to think about who she might have fucked. The thought made me want to find and kill every male who had touched her.

"You might have better control. You're a stronger person than she was. She was my mother and tried her best, but she wasn't prepared for raising a baby tiger without help. She did the only thing she knew how." She tugged at the hem of my shirt and looked down at her knees.

"I don't think we should risk it when we have all this delicious prey in a closed environment." She reddened and huffed out a breath of annoyance. "When I first came aboard, I sized up all the crew members I saw to pick out which ones I'd eat first. My tiger thought you had an embarrassment of riches in your choice of suitable prey."

I winced. "You shouldn't tell them that."

Choking out a laugh, she said, "You think?"

"Who did you choose for the first?" The question was moot, of course. I knew she wouldn't hurt a soul on my battle cruiser unless someone was stupid enough to provoke her. But I wanted to know her thought processes.

"Your steward. He's young and tender. I would have taken Merkella to prevent her from stealing food meant for my cubs and to keep her away from my mate."

Listening to her reasoning delivered in that flat, wary voice, I knew she was right. There was too much risk involved for us and my entire crew. Sighing in disappointment, I said, "All right. No biting until we reach Ximera."

"Thank you for understanding. Should we go talk to the Krenion now? We always seem to get distracted, and I want this done."

"No," I said as I stood and pulled her to her feet. "We'll have breakfast with the first councilor so you can share this additional information. After that, we'll talk to the Krenion."

She frowned, but nodded. "Could we do breakfast after? Fengar likes to hear himself talk and always wants to rub my belly. I don't mind, but it tickles, and he always manages to catch my kick reflex. It's embarrassing."

A growl rose in my throat, and I pulled her into my arms. "No male will ever touch you like that. I won't permit it." I tried to sound fierce, but I had to hide a grin at the thought of her kicking like a *penaka* getting its tummy rubbed.

"You almost sounded like a tiger just now."

"Did you like it?"

Her lips twitched into a shy grin. "Yeah. I really like it."

I picked her up. With a squeal, she wrapped her legs around my waist, hooking her ankles at my back. Her arms snaked around my neck, and she inhaled. Her lips parted as she took my scent into her lungs. I wished I could do the same but had to be content with the odor of grass and slightly metallic water from the lake. It wasn't her personal scent, but the odors would always remind me of her.

"Maybe we can hold off on breakfast," I said, nuzzling her neck. Darting my tongue out to the skin of her throat, I tasted her. She was sweet and delicious with just a hint of salt. I groaned as she squirmed against my hard cock, and her hot wetness stained the front of my pants.

I took two long strides and pushed her against a tree, kissing her. Stars, she tasted like everything I'd ever wanted. Sweet and spicy and warm. I sucked her tongue into my mouth, caressing it with mine. Her hands fumbled at the fastening on my pants, and I considered pushing her away. As if she'd heard my thoughts, her claws extended, and she ripped my pants open to allow my cock to spring free.

I spared a brief thought for getting back to my quarters with my dick wet from making love to her, but pushed the image away as she lowered herself on my throbbing cock. When I touched her hot center, I couldn't think at all. Although I'd told her we wouldn't consummate our relationship until we could announce our mating to the Council, I decided it wasn't necessary. To my mind, we were already mated.

Sinking my hand into her soft mane, I tugged her head back and nibbled at her neck. Could I bite her once I got my tiger? I didn't know, but I wanted to leave my mark on her more than I wanted my next breath. Her needy whines were music in my ear, and I bit down hard, relishing her scream of pleasure mixed with pain.

She clamped her inner walls so hard I saw stars, and I felt a gush of her sweet wetness bathe my cock as she shook with her orgasm. With a growl, I shifted her against the tree, changing my angle of penetration to catch the roughened flesh in her channel that would increase her pleasure.

"God, please, Rakon!" Her claws scraped my back, and I roared as I sank my flat teeth into her shoulder, holding her hair to keep her still for my bite. I clamped my teeth hard, knowing I would leave a bruise everyone could see.

Her head fell back, and she submitted. I hadn't known I'd wanted it until she willingly bared her throat to me. With a growl, I bent my knees to thrust even harder as my balls tightened, drawing up into my belly as I prepared to release inside her.

But I wanted to mark her with my scent. I pulled out and let her go, watching in satisfaction as she dropped to her knees, panting out her release. I stroked myself as she gazed up at me, her lips parted, and she watched avidly as I fisted my cock. With a growl, I came, spraying my cum all over her face and chest. I dropped to my knees and pushed her until she sprawled against the tree, eyes wide and lips parted in surprise.

I gripped her hips and lifted her to my mouth. I wanted her scent on me almost as badly as I'd wanted mine on her. I wanted her juices running down my chin.

CHAPTER
EIGHT

RENATA

I couldn't do anything but pant and whine as he lifted my hips to his face. He devoured me, his tongue licking my folds, growling as he sucked and bit at my flesh. His attention was almost painful in its intensity and I screamed in delight as he thrust two thick fingers into my pussy. I loved the feel of his stubble on my thighs.

I hadn't minded him spraying me with his cum. It was messy and wet, and I shivered as it dripped from my chin, but we liked smelling like him. We liked having his mark on us. We fucking loved having his bite. No other male would dare touch us with his scent embedded in our skin.

He sat up, yanking my hips forward until he could impale me once more with his cock. I couldn't believe he'd gotten hard again so quickly. I tried to wrap my thighs around his waist, but he growled and pressed my legs to my chest, opening me to his use. His heavy body pinned me to the simulated forest floor, and I relished the sensation of hard-packed dirt against my back and a harder male against my front.

Fangs dropped into our mouth, the sting of the eruption lost in the pleasure coursing through our body. We wanted to bite him so badly. Fluid from the mating gland dripped to our tongue, making us drool in anticipation of the taste of our mate's blood.

I'd had sex a few times with human males, but none had ever made our fangs drop. Not once had I ever felt such an overwhelming need to bite. I forced my head to the side, closing my mouth to prevent any accidents. Rakon grabbed my hair, forcing me to look at him as he fucked me.

"Bite me! I want it right now, mate."

"We can't! Rakon, we have to wait!"

He ignored my cries and pushed my face into his flesh where his neck met his shoulder. It was the place I'd imagined that I would set my bite. A taste wouldn't hurt.

We licked his shoulder, tasting him. He was so delicious, and we scraped his skin with the tips of our fangs.

No! We couldn't bite! We were too far from Ximera! But my tiger took the decision away, and Rakon roared in pain and pleasure as we sank our teeth deeply into his flesh.

His salty-sweet, delicious blood coated our tongue, and we purred as the fluid from the mating gland poured into his body. His cock thickened, and he thrust harder than ever, touching my cervix as he filled me to bursting with his cum. I cried out around the flesh and muscle in my mouth as another orgasm washed over me, more powerful than the last.

I could feel the gland empty and recede into my body. It was like having a bad tooth that was somehow relieved. My body realized the wrongness only when it was removed. I couldn't control my whimper, a mix of pleasure, fear, and relief. I was feeling all those things, but I also sensed my mate.

Not his thoughts, of course. I sensed *him*. I would always know where he was in relation to me. We would always be able to find each other. My canines receded, and I licked the wounds I'd left. He would carry the scar forever.

Once I'd cleaned his blood and sealed the wound, I said, "I hope we didn't make a mistake, love. I'm sorry I—"

"Do. Not. Apologize. Not ever. Do you understand?"

His throaty growl made me want to start our play all over again but I had to focus. "I wasn't going to apologize for biting you. I was going to apologize for not being able to control myself long enough to wait until we reached Ximera."

"I wanted it."

"We aren't cubs, Rakon. We can wait for things, and we'd decided to wait until we got home."

His dark eyes flashed yellow, and I knew he would shift soon. "Plans change, mate. Now take off my shirt. I want everyone to see how I've marked you." He glared proudly at the bruises and scratches marring my legs, and stripes stained his face.

"Shit!" I leaped out of the way of his hand, but his clawed fingers caught the fabric of his shirt, and he shredded it like paper. "Computer!"

He roared, the concussive sound rattling in my ears as fur sprouted on his arms and face. I'd never expected it would happen so quickly or I'd never have allowed him to touch me. I knew I had only a few minutes before he lost his lucidity entirely.

"Computer!"

"Do you have an instruction, War Mate Renata?" I nearly sobbed in relief at the digitized voice and dashed around a tree, out of reach of Rakon's claws.

"Message to Patrek. Do not enter the holo under any circumstances. No one is to enter the holo! Seal the door!"

"Message delivered and received by Science Officer Patrek. He asks if you need assistance."

"No!"

Another roar sounded in the cold air of the sim, and I knew I'd run out of time. Even in his half-shifted form, he was a beautiful male. Yet he needed help. We remembered our first time. It had been hell making the leap into the tiger's body. The human wanted to retain the things that made up a human. Bipedal locomotion, color vision... thumbs. A four-legged animal is an alien thing to a humanoid. It might have been better if I could talk to him, but I wasn't sure he had enough lucidity to listen to words.

"I can see you, mate. Tell me what to do."

His amber eyes were filled with pain and indecision as he held that half state between humanoid and animal. I hoped he could keep that little bit of rationality long enough for me to try to help him. I knelt by his head.

"You have to let go, Rakon. You have to let him inside and let him show you what to do. You're stuck halfway."

He grimaced in pain as his bones shifted under his skin. "Don't... understand."

"You're trying to retain your rational thought, but you can't. You have to give up control to him."

He panted hard and squeezed his eyes shut as his tiger pushed for control. "This hurts, Renata. I can't stop—"

"Don't stop! You wanted this so badly you made me bite you before we were ready. Now cowboy up and deal with your shit, Warlord! And get on with it. I'm late for breakfast."

He blinked at me in shock, his mouth hanging open. Sendra had always said that when I'd complained about something. I didn't know what it meant, but it seemed appropriate for this moment. And it worked. His first shift was painfully slow, as mine had been, but within a few minutes, I saw his tiger.

And what a glorious orange beast he was! Larger than me by a few hundred pounds, he was the size of one of the small cars that littered the streets of Atlanta. He lay on the ground, limbs twitching as he recovered from his ordeal. I wished I had something to feed him, but I wasn't willing to go for the second stasis container until he was calm and stable.

Yet within minutes, he was asleep, stretched out on his side and snoring. I held in my laughter as I tiptoed to the door. Unfortunately, I couldn't go out. I had pants around here somewhere, but he'd ripped away the shirt I'd worn.

"Computer," I hissed, trying to keep my voice down.

"Would you like me to whisper, War Mate Renata?"

The voice boomed through the sim, and I winced as I glanced back at Rakon. "Yes, damn it! Whisper. Soft, inside voice, please."

"Of course, War Mate. Do you require assistance?"

The voice was softer, but still too loud. "Have someone bring clean clothes to the holo. Tell them to leave them just inside the door, but they should not enter. I also want more meat."

"Message delivered and received, War Mate. Do you require further assistance?"

"No. Go away and be quiet!"

"Understood."

I really didn't like computers. I failed to see how a digitally rendered voice could sound so... supercilious. I rubbed my face, the exhaustion of the last few days catching up with me as I trudged back to Rakon's prone body.

I wanted a nap. I wasn't going to hang out at the door waiting for clothing, so I decided to get comfortable and try to rest while Rakon slept off his first shift.

RAKON

I'd always tried to be adult enough to admit when I'd made a mistake. Everything had gone perfectly well until... well, more than perfectly well. I'd never come so hard in my life as I did with my beautiful genetic mate. We'd gotten a little carried away, but what could it hurt?

Bite now, or later? I'd decided now was better. Get it over with, rip off the med dressing, take that step into the future. Renata had been right. Devastatingly right, but I'm not sure it would have been a good experience on Ximera, either. One minute, we were conversing. We were talking about...

I didn't remember. All I remembered was being attacked from the inside by something that wanted out, and that my neck ached like someone had set fire to it. I remembered Renata yelling at me.

Us. Our mate yelled at us because you're slow.

I stiffened at the alien voice speaking in my head. "Who are you?"

I am what you sought. I am tiger.

"Did you come from Renata?" I wasn't sure why I was conversing with the thing, but he seemed to know more than I did. It chuckled at my thought, and I realized it was indeed sharing space in my head, just like Renata described.

No, from you. She just helped me get out.

The creature paced for a moment, and I got a glimpse of amber eyes and black-and-orange stripes before it disappeared into the recesses of my skull. I would never get a straight answer from the beast.

I looked down at Renata. She lay curled up on her side with her hands tucked under her chin. I wanted to wake her so we could talk, but I needed time to adjust. My vision had changed, as well as my sense of smell and hearing. Though colors were muted, I saw details that I'd never noticed before.

The skin of Renata's face was velvety soft. I saw the fine-grained pores, and she had tiny freckles. Her breath whispered softly from her parted lips and I heard her heart beat strong in her chest.

And the scent of her. It was a mix of our sex and her own personal perfume. I knew I'd never forget that delicious fragrance. I smelled her general health. She wasn't in peak condition, but she was better than she'd been when I'd found her.

I held out a hand and tried to extend my claws as I'd seen her do in medical.

Our claws. Ask and I might help.

"Would you..."

Just think about it, lesser male. I can hear very well.

I grimaced and pictured what I wanted. A few seconds later, my right hand bore six-inch claws sharp enough to tear through a stasis container. But my tiger was an insolent beast, and I knew I'd have to teach him better manners.

I'd like to teach you to be smarter, but I doubt either of us will get what we want, lesser male.

"Infuriating creature."

As our mate said, cowboy up and deal with your shit. You asked for a tiger.

I was not going to win this fight. I pictured us taking a swim, and before I'd completed the thought, our paws settled deeply into the leaf litter as we made our way to the lake. As we swam, we knew we'd made the right decision to accept the change.

That wasn't to say that there wouldn't be a period of adjustment. Renata had said that her animal was a creature of instinct, seeking only to meet the most basic of necessities to continue her survival and procreation.

Feed, fight, and fuck. In that order, the tiger supplied, not helpfully.

I scowled. Mine seemed to be more intellectual and self-aware, and possessed a dry, caustic wit I wasn't sure I liked.

You're not human, idiot. Did you not think there would be differences?

We strode from the water and shook the liquid from our fur before dropping to our back for a good roll in the dry sand. It felt amazing, and we groaned in pleasure as we rubbed our muzzle against the pebbles littering the beach.

Our mate is waking up. She'll want to speak.

I'd felt a tinge of something, an awareness, perhaps, but I hadn't realized what it was. I watched her roll over and sit up, blinking against the sunlight as she looked for me. The tiger gave me a push, and we flowed into our human form and strode forward to greet the sum of our happiness.

I hunkered down next to her and kissed her cheek. "I'm sorry."

"What for?" A small smile played about her lips, and I reached over to kiss her again.

"You were right, and I'll probably have to apologize every day for the rest of our lives. We should have waited."

She frowned, the skin between her arched brows wrinkling. "I'm not sure how you're managing to stay lucid, but I'm not complaining. Are you okay?"

"Define okay." I grimaced, and the tiger chuckled darkly.

"Are you ill or otherwise unwell?"

"No, but I am confused. I thought my tiger would be more..." I rubbed a hand through my hair. "I thought we would be more animal, but he reminds me of the first councilor."

"What? He reminds you of Fengar?"

"He's sarcastic and has too much to say."

Her eyes widened. "Stop insulting him! He can hear you, you know."

I received an angry huff and had the impression of a furry tail waved in my face. I winced, knowing the tiger was not amused. "Sorry. I don't know how to explain it. He says it's because I'm not human."

"Oh." She looked down at a tuft of grass and played with it. "I suppose I hadn't thought of that, but it makes sense that an animal hosted by a Ximeran would be different. You're a lot bigger than I expected, for one thing. What other differences are there?"

"I have no idea how much of the animal he retains. Is he simply a tiger in shape but carrying the higher mental processes of a Ximeran or human? If so, to what degree?" I winced and shook my head. "Oh, no. I am not telling her that, hairball!"

"Hairball? Is that what we're calling them now?" Tears of mirth sparkled in her eyes, and she tried to hide a smile behind her hand.

"No, he said... never mind. The important thing is whether or not we feel I'm safe to be around my crew."

She glanced up at the replicated sun. It represented time on the ship, though lacked the accuracy of conventional timepieces. "Well,

I'd say we could give it a try. Frankly, you've gone through the process weeks faster than I did." She scowled. "Months, really. I didn't talk much afterward. I'm a little jealous."

I stood and held out a hand to help her to her feet. "Do you want to try to make it to our quarters?"

"Yes, but first I want to know what he said." She set her feet and refused to move.

"No, you really don't."

"Tell."

I sighed and let go of her hand, careful to keep some space between us. I had claws now, but she was likely to bare her own at what the hairball had said about her tiger. "He said that we were more highly evolved, and therefore superior."

Her eyes narrowed, and I backed away, unwilling to tell her the rest.

"And?"

Shit. My shoulders rounded into a slump. "And that it was customary for the male to be smarter and stronger than the female," I whispered. "But I don't believe it for a second."

"I believe it's time for our first lesson, Warlord." When I opened my mouth to object, she waved her hand. "Not for you, for the hairball. There is a container of meat and clothing near the exit. If you can reach it and pin me, you may have it."

"What happens if you pin me?"

"You go hungry. I'll give you a head start and allow you to shift first. You should run as soon as you are able." Her small foot tapped the ground, and she crossed her arms.

"All right." I turned my attention to my tiger. "You got us into this mess. A little help would be nice."

You are unwise. You should not share my words. In fact, you should spank her for disagreeing with you.

Oh, fuck no. While the thought of spanking her luscious ass was enticing, it was asking for trouble. She might enjoy our games in bed, but she was a formidable opponent, as the crew from that Mendaran cruiser could testify... if they were alive, of course.

When the tiger sniffed at my thought, I said, "We are mates. We will share everything. I suggest you keep that in mind. Besides, if you're so superior, you should have no trouble reaching the container and pinning her."

He didn't reply, but I hadn't expected him to. He pushed forth, and we flowed into the body of the tiger. The tip of Renata's tail was already vanishing into the underbrush by the time we'd finished.

Shit.

She'd been more than fair. She'd given us time to shift instead of immediately trying to rip our head off for the insult. We didn't waste any more time and chased after her.

Unfortunately, she'd vanished. Her scent permeated the holo and tracks doubled back on each other, evidence of the many times she'd taken the path. Human prints scuffed the trail until it was unrecognizable.

We trotted through the woods, casting our head back and forth as we searched for her spoor. We were so focused on the trail, the attack on our tender haunches came as a complete surprise. She swiped her deadly claws across our backside, rolling us to the dirt as she dashed away. Her chuffing laughter echoed through the holo, disguising her location.

Roaring in anger, we darted back the way we'd come, farther from the prize, but closer to our mate. When we reached the lake, a massive shove sent us into the water. Rolling and spitting in rage, we sprang to our feet, but she was already gone.

I was losing control of my tiger. He was so enraged he didn't listen when I told him she was baiting us and that we should go straight to the container and ignore her antics. We would lose, but I wasn't sorry. The hairball needed a little humility. He hissed at my thought, but ignored everything else as we leaped forward, determined to find and pin our mate.

She led us all over the holo, and we were growing tired by the time she took mercy on us and herded us toward the container. I didn't know how she'd managed it, but we found her sitting primly next to the pile of clothes, her paw resting proprietarily on the top of our breakfast.

Mine, my tiger growled.

I didn't bother to reply. He'd learn soon enough. I just hoped she'd been right about us being able to heal when we shifted again. When he leaped for her, I sat back and watched.

She roared and met us over the crate, fangs and claws flashing as she bowled us over. She kept her claws away from our most vital parts, but her teeth drew blood many times as she easily flipped us to our back and grabbed our throat, her jaws slowly cutting off our air.

After one hard squeeze to remind us of our hasty words, she let us go and shifted. We lay there, panting in exertion and humiliation. Despite our size advantage, she'd kicked our furry ass.

"Who's superior now, hairball?" I asked.

Our mate is, but we're still smarter.

I let him keep his delusions.

She squatted down and pinched our ear. "Is your tiger satisfied I'm suitably evolved?"

We tried the low rumble we'd heard her use when she was pleased with something, hoping the wonderful sound would make her less angry. It started off as a growl, but we soon had the proper adjustment of our throat muscles and air flow that was necessary to create the pleasing vibration. I wondered what it was called.

It's purring. But tigers do not purr.

There was little point in attempting to point out the error in my tiger's reasoning. But it made our mate laugh. Slapping our hip, she got to her feet and dressed. She picked up the stasis container, leaving the remaining clothes for us.

"You can eat when you can manage to shift." Without another word, she left us in the holo.

Our mate is mean.

"You insulted her." I smirked and decided to rub a little acid into the tiger's ego. "Cowboy up and deal with your shit."

My tiger grumbled and went silent, moving into the back of our shared head as I figured out how to shift into my Ximeran form without his help. Life was about to get very interesting and despite my irritation with him, it was going to be entertaining.

We'd had our fight and our fuck. Now it was time to feed. And then fuck again.

After that, we would take our mate home and make her happy.

CHAPTER

NINE

RENATA

My tiger curled up in the back of my head, purring happily. We had chosen wisely in our mate. He was a fearsome orange creature and would give us many fine cubs. Though they were untaught, Rakon and his tiger would soon learn what it meant to be mated to the Panteris.

I loved the markings on his tiger's face. The swirls of black and orange matched the brand on his Ximeran form. I didn't know if it was his tiger's doing, or if it was some genetic anomaly present in Ximeran DNA that gave him such a unique stripe pattern, but I adored it.

His seed trickled from my core, dampening the crotch of my pants. My body ached from his possession, but it was the most delicious of hurts. Though I hadn't come to Rakon untouched, sex with him was like nothing I'd ever experienced. Was that how it was between mates? I could barely fathom such a thing. If it was true, I'd be lucky to survive the surfeit of pleasure. I let out a gasp as my pussy twinged. Even though I was sore and aching, I'd lift my tail if he so much as crooked one of those winged eyebrows at me. I wanted several leisurely days to explore my new mate and growled low in anticipation.

I reached our den, declining several offers of assistance along the way. After a night in fur and Rakon's depredations, I had a pretty good idea what I looked like and didn't blame the crew for their concerned attention. Leaving the stasis container just inside the door, I fiddled with the comm. Fengar had told me of something he called pancakes and I wanted to try them. He'd described them as a chemically leavened bread that had been a common breakfast food on old Earth, served with a spreadable fat and a sweet liquid he'd called maple syrup.

Wasn't maple a kind of tree? How did a sweet liquid come from a tree? Maybe Patrek would know.

Even though it was far past time for a morning meal, the galley attendant agreed to my request. I sat down to wait and clicked on the vidscreen. Several messages awaited, but most were for Rakon. I left those alone. I had one from Fengar and another from Patrek. I tapped the screen to let them know I'd returned to our quarters.

To my surprise, I had one from Magistrate Smith. He apologized for allowing me to be stolen and asked after my health. It wasn't his fault though. The one I really wanted was Jensen, but he'd vanished.

It took me several minutes to reply. I could read well enough, but writing was always a challenge. Since Magistrate Smith's message was written, I wanted to reply in the same way, although an audio recording would have been much easier.

I could never think about how the words went together and struggled putting my thoughts in order on a comm. It was a little embarrassing, but I was more fortunate than most. I'd had Sendra to teach me the basics. If it hadn't been for her, I probably wouldn't have learned to read at all. Literacy had become a lost art when I'd been a cub.

A chime sounded at the door, and I clicked the comm absently, still lost in thought. Fengar's booming voice drew me out of my funk.

"There's my Renata! Where's your mate, child?"

I smirked, wondering how long it would take Rakon to remember he had thumbs. "He's likely still in the holo."

He sat down on the couch next to me, propping his cane against the cushions. "May I ask what that evil smile is for?" He grinned in delight. "You simply must share the nefarious deeds you've been plotting."

I laughed helplessly. Fengar must have had many women fighting over him in his day, the old charmer. "I'm not plotting anything, but I do have further information about how Ximerans will tolerate their mate's bites."

Leaning forward expectantly, he said, "Go on."

"Actually, I have no idea if this will be universal among all males and their mates, but Rakon seemed to have a much easier time coming to terms with his tiger than I'd expected." I described my first adolescent shift and contrasted it with Rakon's.

He stroked his chin thoughtfully. "Do you think your difficulty was because you were a child?"

"I don't know. By the time I was old enough to shift, there wasn't anyone alive who might have known. My mother was a bitten human, but she never described it to me other than to say she was wild for about a week. Given that we have only Rakon's experience, I don't think it's a good idea to trust the information. For all I know, it may be different for every individual."

"What about your friend? Sendra, right?"

"It never came up. I was an adult and well past my first shift when we met."

The chime at the door sounded again and I clicked the response. The steward came in, smelling of delicious fear as his hands shook under the tray he carried.

"Thank you. You can set it on the table." The odors emanating from that tray made my mouth water. There was something that smelled meaty under that domed lid.

"Yes, War Mate Renata." He set the tray down and beat a hasty retreat before I could get up.

"Stop scaring the help, child," Fengar chided.

"I only scared him once! He had meat and wouldn't give it up."

I heard a low growl from the doorway and a yelp of fear as Rakon pushed past the terrified steward.

"What happened to you?" Fengar's eyes were wide as he took in the bloodstains on Rakon's clothing.

My mate slumped into a chair and lifted the cover off one of the plates. His nose twitched as he inhaled the scent of meat. "Later, old male. Hungry now." His low growl made the crystal water glasses rattle as he pulled the plate closer and began to shovel food into his mouth.

Fengar opened his mouth, his expression tight and forbidding, but I put a hand on his arm. "Let him have a few minutes. His tiger was unwise, and they lost their breakfast."

Blinking in surprise, Fengar muttered, "You'll have to tell me that story later."

"Much later." We waited until Rakon had finished everything on the table. It hadn't been fair of me to deny him meat, but his hairball needed to learn a lesson.

Rakon's eyes cleared and he coughed uncomfortably. "I'll order you more food before I get cleaned up."

"Don't worry about it. I can wait until later. Do you want some help? Some of those bites look bad."

He touched a finger to his bleeding shoulder. "No. The sonics will take care of most of it and I'll try to get that mangy cat to shift again."

I arched a brow. "He's mangy now? I thought he was a hairball."

"Mangy hairball. He's the reason I'm bleeding and hungry." He scowled at me, and I tried to hide a smile.

"The stasis container is by the door. If you can shift now, it's yours."

He grunted and the tiger appeared. It looked like painfully slow going for him. When he'd finished, he examined the container and hooked a claw under the lid. With a powerful jerk, he tore the lid away and started devouring the contents.

"Those things are supposed to be indestructible," Fengar whispered.

We liked Fengar's expression of shocked awe at the sight of our fierce mate. "Not so much. They're easy to open for a tiger, but we should try to remember not to destroy any more. They're probably expensive."

"Very," he said absently, still focused on the hungry tiger by the door.

"Sorry."

My tiger bared her teeth and stretched. *Not sorry.*

I hid my grin behind my hand at my tiger's comment. When he finished his meal, Rakon grunted and padded into our bedroom, his tail twining around my shoulder as he passed. I heard the sonic shower run for several minutes as Fengar and I chatted about the Ximeran sights.

RAKON

Though the mating bite on my shoulder was sore and inflamed, it appeared to be healing. It would leave a nasty scar but I would bear it proudly, knowing it was a visible sign of a fully mated male. Actually, everything was healing. The dozen or so deep bites on my arms and legs trickled blood sluggishly, but most of the minor scratches and cuts from our battle with Renata's tiger were already closed. The pulled hamstring and cracked ribs would take more time.

It was likely she'd have killed me easily if she hadn't been working so hard to avoid hurting me. Ximerans trained for battle from a very early age. When we'd had children on Ximera, a very few gifted ones started as early as six, living with their parents and training with local warriors until they were old enough to go to permanent training facilities at twelve.

Despite a lifetime of combat training, a size advantage of at least fifty kilos, and a well-nourished and honed body, Renata had kicked my ass. It had been a humbling and mortifying experience for both me and my tiger. I might have felt a little better if she'd been trying to hurt me, but the knowledge that she'd been playing stung at my ego.

Shut up, already. We know we made a mistake.

I had to chuckle at my tiger's disgruntled growl. "It's still your fault, hairball."

My War Mate was deadly, and I couldn't be prouder. She might not have an evolved tiger, but she had a survivor. She had a tiger who would protect my cubs. My tiger nodded sullenly, though he didn't reply.

Yet I had to wonder. Her tiger exhibited very advanced tactical skills. Had she simply focused on feed, fight, and fuck for survival? Would her tiger grow intellectually in an environment that encouraged higher reasoning?

You should hope she doesn't. She's very dangerous.

"I know. It's quite wonderful. Perhaps we should learn from her."

I wasn't surprised when the tiger didn't respond, and I finished my shower as quickly as I could. We didn't like leaving our mate alone with another male and I wanted to take her back to bed. Ignoring my thickening cock, I dressed and returned to the main room.

Fengar was too close to our mate. We didn't like it at all, even though the old male was too frail to fight.

I picked her up from the couch, ignoring her irritated sniff as I sat down in a chair, positioning her on my lap. She didn't struggle against my grip, and I realized she knew I was on the edge of violence.

We really should have waited until we reached Ximera.

We should listen to our mate next time.

I refused to answer the mangy hairball.

When the door chimed and Fengar touched the comm to admit Patrek, we let out a low growl. Patrek was young, unmated, and very definitely a threat. The only thing that kept us from open violence toward one of my oldest friends was the scent of my cum on Renata's delectable body.

"I have a gift for War Mate Renata." He held up a silvery wrapped package, but paled and stopped at the door when we growled again.

"Get out. All of you."

His face set in a fearsome scowl, Fengar said, "Commander Rakon, I suggest you have a care with how you speak to me."

We hissed as stripes blossomed on our skin. The tiger desperately wanted to hurt the First for his arrogant words, and it was all I could do to keep him in check. "Do you want to watch me fuck my mate, old male?"

Renata let out a snort of laughter. Turning to Fengar, she said, "You better go, sir. I'm not sure if he's quite got control of his tiger yet."

"I don't want to leave you alone with him, Renata." Glaring at me, he added, "He doesn't look entirely sane right now."

"I'll be fine. His tiger already knows what will happen if he does anything stupid." She stood, and ignoring my tiger's furious growling, helped Fengar out. I stomped over and secured the door behind them, then turned to my beautiful mate as her shirt hit me in the face.

Her grin lit up her face and I caught my breath at the sight. She was so beautiful when she was happy. Though I'd wanted to tear the clothing from her body and rip it into tiny shreds, her seductive tease as she pushed her pants down over her hips held me motionless. In a matter of seconds, she stood naked before me, her shoulders thrust back proudly as her bicolored hair trailed down to conceal her breasts. The dark patch of curls covering her mons glistened with moisture and I opened my mouth to catch her scent.

I'd been worried that she would be frightened of my new nature, but I should have known better. Renata's eyes dilated and her heart rate increased as her arousal filled the air in our den. I inhaled, sucking her decadent fragrance into my lungs. The warmth of her skin heated the air around her and I closed my eyes to better enjoy her presence.

Laughing softly, she said, "Catch me if you can, Rakon."

I opened my eyes and smirked. We wanted to chase, and our mate wanted to run. "It's on, *penaka*."

RENATA

Rakon lunged at me, nearly catching me off guard. Though he was clumsy, he was faster than I'd expected. I jumped as he tried to catch me around my hips, flinging myself out of his reach. Unfortunately, our den didn't have sufficient space for games and his claws grazed my ankle as I escaped.

Ignoring the scratches, I balanced on the balls of my feet, waiting for him to approach. His rumbling purr made me smile as I leaped over his couch, putting the heavy furniture between us. "Only cubs purr in their human shape," I taunted.

"I'm a Ximeran Warlord, not human. It makes you happy, and you smell..." His lips turned up into a Flehmen response, baring sharp fangs. "You smell gorgeous when you're happy." His amber eyes narrowed, the pupils contracting as he focused on me.

Rakon smelled delicious to us too. His scent was a mix of aroused male, our sex, and the sweet fluid from my mating gland. Coupled with his arousal and aggression, it was a heady perfume and I wanted more.

I shrieked when he darted forward and caught me around the waist. He pulled me against his chest, bare and slick with sweat, and I wanted to rub against him to share his scent. I considered struggling free to continue our game, but I was where I wanted to be—clutched tightly in my mate's arms. I turned to face him and jumped, wrapping my legs around his hips as I sank my hands into his hair.

"I win," he growled.

"If you do it right, we both win." I tugged on his hair and kissed him. The taste of my mate was indescribably delicious, and I nipped his lower lip, desperate to taste the elixir of his sweet blood on my tongue. It was an atavistic desire, demanded by my tiger. She purred as we lapped at his essence, drunk from the flavor and scent.

His cock pressed against my core, and I shifted my weight to rub against it. When the wound on his lip sealed, he pulled away and carried me into the bedroom. "I'm going to fuck you blind, mate. I want my seed inside you and I want you to grow fat with my cubs."

He fell to the bed, landing on top of me and stealing my breath. "I should tie you to the bed with your legs spread so I can fuck you until you're pregnant. I'll bind you on your hands and knees so I can spank that pretty ass whenever I want, and I'll feed you good meat from my fingers so you stay strong for my cubs."

I gasped at his words, and at the ridge of his cock pressing against my pussy. The fabric of his pants abraded my tender flesh, but I wanted more. I didn't think he'd been serious, but the thought he might be sent a spike of arousal through my body, making me shudder.

He stood, looming over me as he tore his pants away. His thick cock jutted upward, hard and leaking precum from the tip. I drooled in anticipation of the taste of him, but he had other plans. Rakon pulled my thighs apart and growled as he inhaled, the low vibrations making me shiver.

"Stars, you smell so fucking good." He coughed out a groan of pleasure as he lowered his lips to my needy pussy.

I closed my eyes as he sucked my clit into his mouth, grazing the sensitive bundle of nerves with his teeth. I bucked against the sharp sting of his bite, whimpering in need as he licked me with his roughened tongue. Unlike our mating in the holo, he took his time, his attention languid and slow as if he wanted to savor every drop of my arousal.

It was maddening and I wanted more. I put my hands on his head, my fists clenching in the long strands of his dark hair as I pushed his face into my pussy.

He snarled, the sound sharp and loud in my ears. "Put your hands behind your head or I'll tie them."

Returning the angry sound, I said, "Stop teasing me!" I tugged harder at his hair, desperate for more.

My tiger bumped against me, her sinuous thoughts twining with mine as she said, *Do as our mate says. Be patient and let him feast.*

Whimpering, I obeyed and made my fists unclench, then dropped my hands to my sides. Rakon purred his approval, the vibrations resonating against my wet core.

RAKON

"Open your eyes, Renata. I want you to look at me before I let you come."

Her beautiful face was flushed with pleasure and black stripes danced across her cheeks as I teased her to the brink of orgasm. Her thin body shuddered under my hands as she strove to reach the pinnacle I didn't want to give her. Yet.

Her sweet nectar bathed my face, embedding her unique scent in my skin. We wanted to smell like her, wanted to be so connected that our scents were indistinguishable. I understood her careless nudity now. Although she was incredibly beautiful, it was her scent and taste that drew me. I was entranced by the stripes blushing across her cheekbones, telltales of her arousal and emotions.

Her decadent perfume was like Mendaran brandy on my tongue, intoxicating and potent. I lapped at the generous moisture, wanting to claim every drop for myself. Her come would be infinitely sweeter, and I eased two fingers into her channel, curling them to stroke the roughened spot that would bring her delight.

Renata's screams of pleasure were music as I fucked her with my fingers, pushing her ever closer to completion. Giving one last suck to her delectable clit, I moved up her body, desperate to kiss her as I buried my fingers in her pussy and ground the heel of my hand into her clit. She licked me, swiping her tongue across my lips and chin as she took her own essence into her mouth.

"Please, Rakon! I need to—"

Her eyes closed as she arched her neck. I nipped at the straining tendon in her throat, relishing the pulse of blood rushing through her carotid. "Just a little more," I whispered. "I want to see you beg for it."

I pulled away, watching with satisfaction as her eyes flew open. Her hips moved in tandem with my fingers, deepening the penetration into her succulent flesh.

"Rakon! Please! Please, let me come!"

"Such a good mate you are." I lowered my lips to hers once more, relishing the taste of her.

She moaned into my mouth as I deepened our kiss. I could hear the wet sound of my fingers fucking her. Thrusting even harder, I said, "Come for me, Renata. Give me your pleasure."

She stiffened, her back bowed as her eyes squeezed shut. Her arched brows nearly met in the middle as her face crumpled. She opened her mouth, fangs bursting forth as the tiger's scream of passion echoed. The rippling muscles of her pussy clenched my fingers as I thrust them inside her, prolonging her pleasure.

My cock ached to claim her. I had ignored my need for too long.

As she gasped for air, her fangs receded and she gave me a drowsy smile. "You're amazing. Where did you learn that?"

I tapped her lips and kissed her sweaty forehead. "A warrior never tells, but I'm not done yet."

She screeched when I turned her to her belly and lifted her hips as I positioned myself between her splayed thighs, letting out a groan of utter contentment as I eased my thick cock inside her welcoming pussy. Stars, the sensation of her surrounding me was like nothing I'd ever felt before.

Wanting to be close to her, I lowered my torso until I sprawled over her back. Her striped hair tickled my face and I brushed it aside to set my lips to her tender skin as I fucked her. Her hips met mine, the slapping of our flesh loud in my ears. She arched her back, her sinuous body curving as she met my thrusts.

I would never get enough of my beautiful mate. She was glorious and wild, and all mine.

Bite her. Mark her as ours.

Fangs burst forth and I sank them deeply into the muscle at the base of her neck. She roared and bucked against me. Not to escape, but to deepen the penetration. Claws erupted from my fingertips and I squeezed her hip to keep her still. I wanted to drag out this slow, methodical fuck and make it last as long as I could.

We purred around her sweet flesh, lapping her blood away as our fangs receded. I'd known it would happen, but when the punctures faded from her fair skin, the disappointment was surprisingly acute. I brushed it aside. After all, I had a wonderful mating mark from her.

"Rakon, please don't tease me!"

Her pussy clenched around me as she whimpered. I loved the sounds of her pleasured cries. She shuddered around me as her claws tore my sheets to ribbons in desperation. The scent of her sweat and arousal filled my nose and I opened my mouth to better catch the fragrance of her as I made love to my brilliant mate. She shuddered, her channel tightening until I had to bite my lip to keep from spilling inside her too quickly.

Letting go of her hip, I pushed my hand between her thighs to rub at her clit. With a scream, she let go, coming for me in a rush of slick fluid. I could no longer hold back. My balls tightened, drawing up as my come burst forth and bathed her sweet pussy with my essence. I prayed to the ancient gods that she would become pregnant with our cubs.

Panting, she collapsed under me, her stunning, sweaty body lax against our bed. Careful to keep my full weight off her, I dusted gentle kisses across her shoulders, wanting to taste her velvety skin.

"We liked it when you bit us," she whispered. "I wish…" Her voice trailed off and I touched her soft cheek.

"Me, too. But my mating mark is big enough for the two of us, yes?"

She chuckled softly, her eyes closing as her body relaxed. I settled next to her and pulled her into my arms. I'd wondered about her pronoun usage. Sometimes, it was I, and sometimes we. I understood now. Our tigers were integral parts of our psyches, inseparable from the human or Ximeran. And I could no more live without mine than she could live without hers.

I shook my head, wondering what I'd been thinking to refuse such a gift. I closed my eyes and followed my mate into sleep.

RENATA

A comm chimed, jerking me out of sleep. Rakon held me tightly in his arms as he snored in my ear, the sound a charming mix of purrs and throaty growls. I smiled and snuggled deeper into his embrace, but the comm sounded again.

I groaned and eased myself out of Rakon's arms. Picking up the comm, I considered crushing it, but it wouldn't look very good if the Commander's War Mate did something so infantile.

"Shut that thing off and come back to bed," Rakon slurred from behind me.

I smiled, knowing we shared the same thought. Whatever was on the comm might be important, though, so I tapped it to reveal a message. "Patrek asks if we have time for him. He has something he wants to give me," I said.

Grumbling, Rakon rolled over and sat up. Glancing down at the comm in my hand, he winced. "We should get up. I had no idea we'd slept for so long."

"I'm hungry, too," I said as I stood and stretched. "Can we have more of that pancake thing? I never got to try it."

Rakon's face reddened, and he rubbed a hand over his forehead before giving me a sheepish grin. "I'm sorry I ate your meal. I'll put the order in, and we can shower while we wait."

I thought about it for a moment and shook my head. "No, let's clean up and see what Patrek wants. We can eat after that and have the rest of the day to ourselves."

Wrapping a hand around my throat, he lowered his head to kiss me. His soft lips caressed mine and I put my hands on his shoulders to bring him closer and deepen the kiss. He allowed it for just a moment, then slapped my ass.

"Time to get cleaned up. As you said, we have the rest of the day to play after we deal with my annoying science officer." Grinning, he turned away, presenting his backside to me.

With a growl, I bared claws and swiped at his muscular ass, leaving red marks across his haunch. "Stop teasing me, then."

Laughing, he swung me into his arms and carried me into the lavatory. "All right, War Mate. I'll stop until later when I can have you all to myself."

After we finished cleaning up, he gave me a beautiful blue dress. The hem swirled around my ankles with a swish of soft fabric and the bodice left my arms and most of my upper chest bare. I'd never worn anything so lovely or so wildly impractical before, but I loved it immediately. I didn't have to wear clothes to protect my skin from the toxic atmosphere, nor did I need the protection of armor. And the way Rakon's eyes turned amber when he looked at me stroked my nonexistent vanity.

Rakon answered Patrek's chime at our door, allowing him and Fengar into the room. Patrek's eyes lit with approval at my appearance, making Rakon growl and pull me into his lap.

Shaking his head, Patrek grinned at us. "I'm afraid I have to get back to my research on the wolves, but I have a gift for you, War Mate Renata." He held out the package wrapped in silvery paper he'd tried to give me before, laying it in my hands. It was soft and I couldn't think of what it might be. I'd never gotten a present before.

Slipping a thumbnail under the seam, I pulled the edges apart to reveal my leather jacket. It no longer smelled of sweat and ash. Someone had cleaned it and repaired all the damage the garment had sustained over its many years of service. The zipper worked, and even the ancient USAF patch on the breast had been restitched until it looked like it was new. I shook it out and a drawstring bag fell to my lap.

"The bag contains everything we found in the pockets. I hope nothing is missing. We'll deliver the rest of your belongings after they've been cleaned and repaired."

I shook the contents into my hand and gasped. I hadn't had much; just a few fossils Sendra had given me, some old coins, and a faded picture of my mother. Someone had tried to restore the photo, sealing it in plastic. I smiled wistfully as I stroked the image, remembering when I found the old instant camera and her lazy grin as I'd snapped the picture.

"There was also a small solid-state memory drive hidden in the lining. I took the liberty of transferring the contents to your vidscreen." Patrek handed me a tiny object about the size of my human thumbnail. "Was it your personal diary?"

"I've never seen it before, but this jacket once belonged to my great-grandfather. What was on it?"

"My apologies, War Mate. I thought it was personal and simply transferred the data into a usable format without viewing the contents. Would you like us to leave while you watch it?"

Did I? It was possible the information was personal to someone in my family. "No. If it was important enough that one of my relatives hid it in that jacket, it's important enough for all of us to see."

Patrek nodded and touched the control to begin the vid.

The surprisingly crisp recording sprang to life on the screen, revealing a tigress with two young cubs perched on her lap. An older male cub stood behind her, gazing solemnly at me over her head. The youngest were orange tigers with nascent stripes running through flaming red hair and had amber eyes. The oldest male cub though. If he'd been a girl, I'd have been looking into a mirror.

I didn't know why, but I had a feeling he was looking straight at me, rather than into that camera. Perhaps it was simply a trick of the sunlight streaming through the window behind him.

"Happy Father's Day, Daddy!" Their piercing shouts echoed through the vid, making me smile as I wondered who the lucky male had been. Given the date at the lower right corner of the screen, and the obvious tiger characteristics of the cubs, it had to have been meant for my great-grandfather.

I grinned as I listened to the three imps tell their father about their days in school, show him drawings, and plant wet kisses on the camera. It was poignant and incredibly touching, and I had to wipe away a tear.

Their mother finally spoke up. "All right, monkeys! Time to go outside!"

"We're tigers, Mama! Not monkeys!" The youngest stuck a thumb in her mouth as she toddled after the other two.

The woman sighed as she watched her cubs leave. Yet when she turned to face the camera, her expression had grown hard and remote.

"I have a message from the High Leopard, Panterum. They bid your Panteris to tell you that you need to come home. They bid me to tell you that something is coming, and they need your presence here, along with that of the Lupis and Lupina, Ursis and Ursina, and representatives from the raptors. The Leo and Leoris from South America told us it was a gringo problem and refused to come. Stupid jaguars. I know you like him, but Martinez is a jackass. I don't know how the Leoris puts up with him."

She wrung her hands. "I don't know what to do, Dimitri. Chen Xifeng is here. It must be something big to drag the High Leopard herself out of Tibet. The bears and wolves will arrive tomorrow, and I've got golden eagles on the roof. The African cats chartered a jet for themselves, the hyenas, and the jackals. I can't even imagine how that's going to turn out." She sniffed, disgust evident on her pretty face.

"I can't imagine jackals and hyenas in my home." She shook her head before continuing.

"Something bad is going to happen and I need you to help me." The vid flickered as she choked back a sob. "They want to send the cubs north into Canada, Dimitri."

She breathed out a heavy sigh. "I'm doing okay for now. They haven't let us tell the cubs anything. Theo, Ana, and Marta only know that they have new playmates, and the adults have decided to tell them we're having a party. But I think Theo suspects something." She smiled and sniffed back a tear. "He will be an excellent Panterum when he comes of age. You will be so proud of him."

Scrubbing her eyes with the heels of her hands, she pasted on a smile. "Anyway. That's the message from the High Leopard, darling. You're due to come home soon, but I want to tell you how much I love you." She kissed her fingertips and touched them to the camera as the vid went dark.

"Chen..." I tapped my chin thoughtfully. "Do you think they were ancestors of Daiyu? And what about Soledad? She mentioned Martinez too."

"It's quite likely, War Mate, but I don't know. Earth's genealogical records are nonexistent." Patrek replied.

I nodded and reached out to stop the vid. Patrek shook his head. "There's more. That was only about a quarter of the contents."

"I see." I settled back in Rakon's lap and let the vid continue.

Rakon and I both gasped in shock when the images resumed. The woman who had appeared so happy with her cubs was no more. In her place was a thin, desperate tigress whose stripes never faded from her skin. Instead of a pretty sundress, she wore heavy black body armor and leather. The sleek bob was gone, replaced by a tangled mass of orange and black stripes.

"These videos are intended to be the final record of the Andreyev tigers. Our Panterum is missing, and presumed deceased. I already know he's dead. The heir has disappeared, and if I know my idiot son, he's gone hunting for the old cat."

She swallowed deeply from a whiskey bottle. "I don't know why I drink this shit. Shifters can't get drunk. Anyway. Last record and all that fuckery. Ana and Marta are safe in what used to be one of Canada's provincial parks, but we'll have to move soon. If Theo has managed to kill himself, they are the last two born tigers."

"The wolves and bears are similarly affected. Ursis and Ursina are both dead, but we managed to track and rescue one of their male cubs. The whereabouts of Lupis and Lupina are unknown, as well as that of their three cubs. They were last seen heading west into the mountains."

"We've heard nothing from the Leo or Leoris. I'm assuming they're dead or have buried themselves deeply enough into the bush they'll be safe. Despite my dislike of the Leo, I hope it's the latter."

"Most of the African contingent tried to head south into Florida, but their boat was swept away in the most recent storm. We've had no news of their whereabouts or if they're still alive. I'm counting them dead. It's probably true, and if it isn't, there isn't a thing I can do for them from what used to be Toronto."

She hissed and spat to the side. "Fucking humans. They had Ursina on a spit over a fire while they watched Ursis bleed out." Fangs sprang out from between her lips, and she licked them. "No human in that camp ate that night, but we did. I fed the leader to their cub a bite at a time while he watched us feast. I loved listening to the screams."

She shook her tangled mane and barked out a laugh. "I still have those damned eagles dogging my footsteps. The fucking birds shit all over everything, but I have to admit that they're excellent trackers. If there's game or fish, they can find it."

Taking a long drink from her bottle, she burped before continuing. "Dimitri, you used to paddle my ass when you heard me swear. So, Dimitri, fuck you. Fuck your dedication to the stupid United States Air Force that doesn't even exist anymore. Fuck you for leaving your cubs. Fuck you for giving your son the same sense of purpose and duty that he just had to go out and look for your stupid fucking ass."

She sniffed and I knew she tried to hide her tears from the camera. "And fuck you for leaving me, Dimitri."

The video cut out and I ignored Rakon's growl to shake Patrek's arm. "Bring her back!"

No one said anything, but I saw the sympathy on their faces. The tigress had been talking about my great-grandfather and her pain was a palpable thing, wrenching even from the distance of so many years.

"There's more, War Mate. She was apparently done with that entry."

We waited until the recording started again. I chewed at a thumbnail, both dreading the words and wanting to hear more. I hoped the tigress would tell me her name.

"We've made contact with Lupis and Lupina, courtesy of the eagles. They are safe in the mountains of northern California but intend to make their way to Alaska and possibly across the Bering Strait to Russia. They heard from a dying orca shifter that the Kodiaks have been spotted hunting across the strait."

She leaned back and propped her boots on the table in front of her, lighting a cigarette. "Nasty habit. I'm not sure why I started.

Doctors used to say you took six minutes from your life for every cigarette. The way we're going, I doubt the hour or six I spend smoking will make a damned bit of difference. Anyway, the news was most welcome. I hope the orcas are well, but I can't do anything for them. I probably can't help the Kodiaks either but making contact might be enough to keep their spirits up."

Exhaling, she let out a plume of white smoke through her teeth. "The new Panterum has also returned. He's gotten huge, almost as tall as his father. When he's grown, he'll be a big bastard." She laughed harshly, choking on her cigarette as she wiped her eyes. "He still calls me Mama. Brought me a daughter-in-law, too. Skinny little bitten shifter. Looks like Alice down the rabbit hole. I want to hate her for having been human, but she's the future of our race now." She took another drag and exhaled the words. "If she lives long enough to whelp a few cubs, that is. I don't care if she dies after that."

Laughing, she shook her head. "I have kind of a new friend, too. A jackal followed Theo back to Canada. Sendra and Misty grew up together and those two are thick as thieves. I guess that explains why Misty didn't try to shoot Theo when he showed her his tiger." She took another drag from her cigarette. "I like Sendra though. She's a good hunter and used to be a schoolteacher. She's wonderful with the cubs."

Holy shit! My great-grandmother had known Sendra? Why hadn't Sendra said anything? How could she have kept such a secret from me all the years we'd known each other? I felt betrayed and angry but forced myself to listen.

Her head fell forward and she didn't speak as she finished her cigarette. Stubbing it out on the sole of her boot, she looked up, her eyes haunted. "Theo brought me Dimitri's jacket. I guess Theo talked to some of the men who brought his body back. I'm using the memory stick I sent him to record everything. It has the last video of a happy family."

"He died a hero in the first wave of storms. I wasn't particularly surprised by the hero part or the dead part. I'm born and we always know when we've lost half our soul."

The video hissed out to blackness, and I stared at the empty screen. As of ninety-two years ago, wolves, Kodiak bears, and raptors existed on Earth. Did they still? My great-grandmother's story was heartbreaking and I felt like I'd lived it with her.

"Is there more?"

"Yes, but it won't be very long."

The next clip showed an older tigress who walked with a pronounced limp. Her hair was cropped close to her skull, liberally sprinkled with threads of gray. A long scar started at her jaw and disappeared under a piece of cloth covering one eye. She settled heavily into her chair and sighed in relief.

"Well, I suppose I haven't done such a great job at recording the last of the Andreyev tigers. There hasn't been time. It's been seven years since the last storm hit. I'm no longer Panteris, but everyone seems to come to me for the big decisions even though I always send them on to Misty. If they'd just give her a chance, they'd figure out she's better at it than I ever was. Fuck, if I didn't know better, I'd swear that girl was born instead of bitten."

She chuckled, the sound rattling in her throat. "Color me surprised. I took one look at that West Virginia piece of inbred shit and wrote her off. It's a good thing she likes me or my hide might be lying in front of her fire pit about now."

She coughed harshly and spat on the floor. I saw a tinge of blood in the expectorated fluid and watched as she wiped her mouth on the sleeve of her shirt. I couldn't tell if she was sick or that badly injured.

"I'm too old for this shit. Anyway, I was chatting over tea with Xifeng." She held up her fingers, knobby with arthritis and crooked from old breaks, forming the tortured digits into air quotes. "Nobody has even fucking seen tea in years. We drank boiled water laced with willow bark. It's the best we can do for pain relief these days, but it will run out eventually. Xifeng is doing a little better. She says it's from Tai Chi. The old bitch has thirty years on me, and she'll outlive me."

She leaned forward, her single eye piercing the camera. "She wanted me to record a message. Kind of a fucked-up message if you ask me, but she didn't, so here I am. This message is for Renata Andreyev. I'm told she's my great-granddaughter. Or was, or maybe will be. I don't know. Xifeng says you're going to be important, but that you must leave Earth."

She leaned back and pulled out a hand-rolled cigarette, lighting it with a candle stub. "I have no idea where she thinks you're going to go, but if you're any spawn of mine, you'll have better sense than to stay in this godforsaken pit if there's an opportunity to go elsewhere. I can't stand all that woo-woo shit those damned snow leopards come up with. But the High Leopard is never wrong about anything. I can't even tell you how many times she's moved us out of the way of danger."

Taking a drag from her cigarette, she spun in her chair. "Those fucking humans are dying by the dozen every day, yet we can't keep ahead of them. If they aren't hunting for meat, they're after fur. We all pray for the day they're gone."

"So, Renata... Pretty name, by the way. If you manage to find this recording, get your orange ass off the planet. Maybe you're white like my Dimitri and Theo, but I hope you're orange. It's easier to hide. Xifeng says you need to find the bears and wolves but the other cats will come to you. Some bullshit about born tigers and a new Panterum. I don't claim to understand a word that leopard says."

Scrubbing her face with her palm, she dislodged the cloth covering her ruined eye and I felt sick. The socket was black with infection, unhealed and untreated. Why hadn't she shifted to heal herself? Where had her tiger gone? She was careworn and battle-weary, but she wasn't so old that shifting should have been a problem.

"This is going to be my last transmission, Renata. I'm sorry to leave things like this. I'm sorry I didn't do a better job giving you information. I'm kind of just fucking sorry for everything. I'm using the last of our stored batteries to run the camera. After this, there are no more. We tried to get a windmill set up, but the humans destroyed it within a few days. Ana was heartbroken. She and Marta worked so hard on it."

She turned her face away from the camera. "I wasn't going to say anything about Marta, but I guess it doesn't matter. She had this romantic idea that a boy in the human camp liked her, and she showed him her tiger. We managed to get her hide back before we destroyed their camp. I lost count of the number of shifters we buried."

"Ana refuses to try for such an idiotic thing. I suppose I should be lucky Misty has already given Theo a white cub. Nikolai is a sweet little guy, very solemn like his sire. I hope she throws him a couple of orange ones, but it's time for me to go to ground and I won't see them. Nobody says anything, but we all know I'm too sick to keep taking up our resources. Food and medicine are too valuable, and we have to save them for the ones who can fight and breed."

She choked out a laugh and spat more blood-tinged fluid to the floor. "Assuming we can ever find mates. That isn't looking likely, given what happened to my poor little girl."

"I've got a personal message for you too. The chasm between the races has to end. We fight amongst ourselves almost as much as we fight the humans. I was probably the worst of us back in the day." She huffed out a wry chuckle but broke into another coughing fit.

"Born Panteris, the highest of the high on the shifter food chain. I'm here to tell you, honey, when everybody is starving and the born jackal shares a rabbit carcass with your grandchildren? That shit makes you equal in a fucking hurry. You don't question the hyena medic who treats your battle wounds. It doesn't matter if he's bitten or born, and if he's got morphine, it doesn't matter if he's a fucking hyena either."

She exhaled a plume of white smoke and leaned back in her chair as she rubbed her empty eye socket. "Anyway, last transmission and all. I wanted to tell you to find a way to stop that fuckery. We can no longer afford to be divided. And good luck, Renata. You're going to need that shit."

Before the vid cut off, she gave the camera a toothy grin that reminded me of the woman she'd been before the storms.

CHAPTER

TEN

RAKON

R enata sobbed in my arms as if her heart was breaking. The cat yowled at me to fix it, but I ignored him. There was no fixing Renata's pain.

All our pain. Fengar cleared his throat, suspicious dampness in his eyes as Patrek helped him from his seat and escorted him to the door. I looked at my old friend over Renata's head.

"I'll focus my efforts on the snow leopards and jaguars, Commander," he whispered.

I nodded, dismissing him.

The hairball paced restlessly, irritating the fuck out of me. I snarled at him to stop, but he ignored me, panting out whining growls as we listened to our mate cry. I picked her up and carried her into our bedroom, crawling into bed with her after I'd laid her down.

I pulled her into my arms, trying to give her what warmth and comfort I could as I mulled over what we'd seen. Patrek had been right; the vid had been intensely personal, but it affected every Ximeran male who would go after a shifter mate. Despite her caustic words, Renata's great-grandmother had given us a great deal of valuable information. I hoped we could find her name.

We had a starting point for our search. I wanted to get to work. I needed to speak with the Magistrate from Earth, needed to breathe down Patrek's neck and make him search faster. Well, after I beat the shit out of him for making Renata cry. Inaction didn't sit well with me or the hairball, but our mate needed us right now.

Her crying eased as she drifted into an uneasy doze, but I felt her tiger's watchful presence like an itch in the back of my brain. She seemed content enough to let me hold Renata, but still guarded her human. I wondered if the tiger ever rested.

We rest when the human is safe and not in distress.

The cat's voice was subdued, and he'd ceased rattling around in my skull. I sent him a soft growl of thanks as I tucked our mate's head under my chin, inhaling the sweet scent of her musk. I couldn't do anything immediately useful, so I closed my eyes and tried to plan how I would transport all available males to Earth to take part in the search.

Yet after less than an hour, her eyes sprang open and she scrambled from the bed. Her face was pale and her eyes were still red from crying, but she looked like a very determined War Mate.

"I'm going to get clean, and then we need to talk. Actually, come with me. We can talk while I bathe."

I shook my head and followed her into the lavatory, watching as she dropped a trail of clothing on her way. I had to readjust my cock in my pants as her bare ass twitched in front of me. Now was not the time, but the thing had a mind of its own.

"What's on your mind?"

"The jackals. There was one living in old Atlanta, so we know at least some of the passengers on that boat my great-grandmother mentioned survived to reach the coast. It's likely to have been South Carolina or northern Florida."

"You don't think they made it down the peninsula?"

"They might have, but it's been flooded for fifty years and laced with toxins from the old oil refineries surrounding the Gulf. They wouldn't have stayed. If there are any of the African shifters left, they'll be somewhere in that region." She huffed out a short laugh. "If I'd known they were that close, I'd have gone looking for them myself."

"Okay, so that leaves—"

She cut off the shower and stepped out, running a hand through her tangled hair. "Pretty much everyone else, although we do have a lead on the wolves, and possibly the Kodiak bears. We need to look up images of the animals so the Ximerans know what to look for."

I followed her from the lavatory and sat on the bed as she dressed. "I've got Patrek stepping up the research on the snow leopards and jaguars."

"That's the other thing. I think we need to focus our attention on finding Chen Daiyu."

"Why not the shifters who remain on Earth?" I asked. "She probably is in imminent danger, judging by how you were treated, but it seems to me we can focus our efforts on Earth and save more than one shifter."

"I'm not saying that we shouldn't look, but my great-grandmother said some things about the snow leopards that made me think." She paused as she pulled the shirt over her head. "Do you have people who deal with religion on Ximera? I can't remember what they were called on Earth, but I think the snow leopards served that purpose for shifters."

She shook her head. "One of them knew my name from almost a hundred years in the past. It's creepy and disconcerting, and I know she's probably the most important person we need to find."

"Yes, we call them Soul Guides, though I've never met one who could tell the future. They perform joinings, funerals, and give advice to any who ask for it. Actually..." I scratched my head as I thought. "I think one of them did recommend Earth as a source of potential mates, so maybe I'm wrong about them being able to tell the future."

Tugging the shirt down to cover her belly, she said, "Let's go find

Patrek and Fengar. It's time to start planning our invasion. I want this thing planned out to the last detail before we present it to your Council."

I groaned at the thought of trying to convince that group of stubborn old men to do anything. "Don't count on their acceptance. They'll argue you into an early grave just to hear themselves talk."

Her expression turned hard and fierce, and I saw the shadow of her great-grandmother in her beautiful face as we walked toward Fengar's suite. The door slid open at our approach. "The Council will learn that no one argues with a tiger on a mission, Commander. They will learn peacefully, or they will learn bleeding. I don't care either way."

I was torn between wishing we'd been a little slower so Fengar hadn't heard her words, and wishing I had a vid to catch his expression. Her great-grandmother would have been proud of the female our mate had become. I had to move behind her to hide my thickening cock from the first councilor. Her throaty growl made me want to whisk her back to our quarters and give her something to scream about.

"I hope you don't include me in your bloodthirsty plotting, War Mate." The First's voice was soft, but chiding.

She grinned and patted his shoulder, her claws pressing gently into the muscle. "Only if you prove to be stubborn."

RENATA

Fengar was sharply intelligent, and I had to work hard to keep up and stay focused on what I wanted. Unfortunately, part of what I wanted wouldn't be possible, and the other part would take time to implement. My tiger chuffed irritably at the delay. We didn't want to talk. We wanted the snow leopard and every shifter still on Earth safely on their way to Ximera.

We eventually hammered out a plan the Council might accept without too much argument or bloodshed. It meant dividing our forces, but it couldn't be helped. Fengar flatly refused to allow more than a certain number of warriors to leave Ximera. I understood his worry though. We all knew the Krenion weren't extinct, and he was trying to protect his home world. I would have done the same thing in his position.

That led me to another question. "I want to see the Krenion who captured me."

"No." Rakon's automatic refusal made my fangs drop and I pushed them back with an angry hiss.

"Care to tell me why?" I smirked, and added, "It's not like he can hurt me. He's just a torso, and I have every intention of ending his miserable life after I make him tell me what I need to know."

Fengar chuckled. "Boy, you're going to lose this fight. I suggest you give her what she wants before she breaks something. Like you." He hauled himself to his feet, and I held out a hand to steady him as he reached for his cane. "I'll come with you."

We trooped to medical, nodding at the guards posted in front of the secured chamber containing the injured Krenion. We bared our fangs in a smile at his whimper of recognition. We liked the scent of terror wafting from his mangled body. And we loved knowing we were the ones who put him in that condition in the first place.

"War Mate Renata and the first councilor have questions for you, Krenion. You will answer them truthfully." Rakon's voice was flat and stern as he spoke, and he glared straight into the terrified eyes of his people's most dire enemy without flinching.

I was so proud of him for that, and I had every intention of rewarding him later with my mouth stretched around his thick cock. The thought made me drool and I licked my lips in anticipation. First, the Krenion, and then pleasure.

"Who shared my information with Norkad?" I wanted to start with an easy one, a question he could lie about.

"N-no one."

"Lie." I sat down on the bed next to him and traced an extended claw down the staples sealing his chest shut from the last time we'd seen each other. "I can smell lies, you know. When you say something that isn't true, your body chemistry changes, along with your heart rate and temperature. Try again."

His throat clicked and he snapped at me but wasn't able to reach far enough to sink his teeth into my hand. I patted his cheek and he turned red with anger. "Mutant bitch," he hissed.

Rakon growled and stripes burst out on his face. I roared, the sound too loud in the small room. "Mine," I said. With some effort, I managed to calm myself enough to speak and turned back to the Krenion. "Try again, and don't piss me off."

He whimpered in terror, knowing he faced more than me. "It was Councilor Harkon," he whispered. "He—"

Fengar gasped, his expression thunderous. "He's lying! No Ximeran would—"

"Lie. You say only part of what you know, but I believe you about Harkon. Tell me why Norkad wanted the shifters, and I'll let you die easily when we reach Ximera."

The Krenion shook his head, his expression suddenly weary and sad. I smelled the change; he'd given up. "I don't know. Not with any degree of certainty. Harkon said that he wanted you and the other mutants for someone else who would pay him enough to retire to sector two in luxury. If we had known what you were..." He trailed off and turned away.

I really had to get a handle on the Ximeran sectors one of these days. "Truth. Do you know if Harkon or Norkad knew of our gifts?"

"It's likely, but I don't know firsthand. Harkon only told us what to look for in the genetic samples of Earth females. If he'd known, he would have warned us to contain you more securely or force you into a stasis chamber. I know Norkad knew, and I suspect he contacted Harkon first."

"Truth. Do you know the location of Chen Daiyu or Soledad Martinez?"

"My brother was to have delivered the Chen female. I can only assume he's dead, given what you did to my crew."

I laughed softly. "If you had left me alone instead of drugging me, you wouldn't have roused my tiger. I wouldn't have known the difference between one transport and the next. Perhaps your brother was wiser or less cruel."

The Krenion huffed out an irritated breath but didn't respond to my bait. "We delivered the Martinez females almost a cycle ago. One of them had a reaction to the drugs, and we put her in stasis until we reached sector seventeen and loaded her on another transport. We got our money, and I didn't bother to ask Norkad what happened to her. If no one treated her reaction to the drugs, she's probably dead. As far as I know, the other two were delivered to their buyer."

"Do you know the identification of that transport?"

"No. The stasis unit was unloaded and taken to another location. We didn't see it and I don't know the identity of the buyer."

"Did you have assistance from Earth?"

"A human called Jensen was our contact. He let us know whenever a mutant turned up during testing, but we didn't involve anyone else."

"I suppose it would have been difficult to find help since you're supposed to have been eradicated from Ximeran space."

He grimaced. "For what it's worth, I'm sorry we got involved with this mess. There are so few of us left and we just wanted enough money to get ourselves out of Ximeran territories." Closing his eyes, he added, "We can't spend money if we're all dead. Mercenaries always forget that part."

Truth. It wouldn't save his life, but his words bought him an easy death. I only wished he'd known more, but it was obvious he was only hired help, contracted to deliver an item without too many questions. I walked out past the guards who glanced at me, wariness in their stares, ignoring Fengar and our mate.

I needed time to think. Between one step and the next, I shifted. The cat wasn't logical; she had little higher reasoning. But she did have exceptional instincts that had kept us alive on a dying planet. I needed her guidance before I could make sense of the information the Krenion had given me. And well before we had to tolerate the presence of Harkon.

A male saw us coming and slapped at the control panel on the holo, dashing away before we reached the door. We needed the peace of the sim to think.

RAKON

Renata trotted down the corridor, scattering my crew in her wake. She'd left a pile of discarded clothing in the middle of the corridor, and I picked them up. She'd want them later, so I put them just inside the door to the holo without going in.

Our claws twitched and my jaw ached as our fangs erupted. I felt the brush of fur on my arms, but the first councilor clapped his hands in front of our face. We snapped at his fingers, and I was immediately ashamed of our aggression toward the old male.

"Pay attention and leave that female alone," he snapped. "We have things to do."

"I want Harkon confined." I growled at the thought of rending the other male into shreds of flesh and bone.

He ignored me and touched a button on his comm unit. His assistant answered the summons.

"How may I assist you, First Councilor?"

"Close the star ports, effective immediately. No one enters or leaves Ximeran airspace."

"But... why, sir? We can't just close—"

"Tell anyone who asks there are imminent solar storms. Tell them the wormholes are unstable. I don't give a damn what you tell them but close the ports on my order. The only ship allowed in or out will be Warlord Rakon's battle cruiser and only on my order. Is that clear?"

"Yes, sir. May I ask why?"

"No." He slapped the comm, ending the communication.

"You need to confine Harkon," I repeated. I had every intention of getting answers and blood from that duplicitous male.

Fengar chuckled. "I've been trying to learn an old Earth game called chess. It's an interesting exercise in strategy and has the benefit of being played in comfortable chairs over glasses of Mendaran liquor."

"What's your point, Councilor?"

His bushy brows lowered into a frown. "Insolent whelp, pay attention. Harkon thinks he's untouchable because of his position on the Council. I want him lazy and complacent, and I don't want him to have time to destroy any evidence. If I have him confined now, he's going to destroy everything he can get his hands on before we can search it. We've already overplayed our hand as it is when I spouted off about the shifter females."

I knew that! I shook my head, trying to push my tiger back. I knew better than to rush in like we'd wanted. Renata would be so disappointed in us. Fengar's order should have been my first thought. "My apologies, sir. I'm not thinking clearly."

His face softened into a wry grin. "You really should have waited until we reached Ximera."

"My mate tried to tell me that. I didn't listen to her."

"My wife used to say that not listening was a male's greatest fault," he said wistfully.

"I'm sorry, sir."

He shook his head and limped toward the lift that would take us to the bridge. "Don't worry about it. We have to make the best of a bad situation here. You'd best hope that Harkon hasn't covered his tracks."

"Yes, sir." My thoughts wandered as the lift took us upward. I would have to work very hard to control my tiger. He already paced, demanding vengeance for the hurt our mate had suffered. Despite my tiger's arrogant insistence that we were superior, he was just as much a creature of instinct and violence as Renata's.

The lift door slid open and I stepped onto the bridge of my ship. Ximera loomed in the vidscreen and I couldn't help my sigh of relief as I took in the sight of my home planet. We'd be there in a few hours. I couldn't wait to get Renata home and naked in my bed.

"Sir, we've received acknowledgment of our approach from the star port. They will wait for the first councilor's order to allow us to dock. Do you wish to respond?"

"Just an acknowledgment of the message, Helmsman." I settled in my chair, smiling as I traced the spoor she'd left on the arm during her first meeting with the full Council. It hadn't gone well, and I doubted that our next confrontation would be any easier. Now that I knew what it was like to rein in my tiger, I hoped I could measure up to her example.

The arrogant hairball inside my head was confident he would remain logical and collected now that we were used to each other. I reminded him I'd barely managed to keep myself under control during my last meeting with the Council. He didn't reply but I knew he considered my words.

"I'm afraid I don't know Councilor Harkon that well, sir. Do you think he's likely to do something rash?"

Fengar gave me a brief smile, then returned his attention to the vidscreen and the planet growing larger by the minute. "Until today, I'd thought he was ineffective at best. I wouldn't have said he'd be capable of such a treasonous act. If Renata is right and the Krenion was telling the truth about his involvement, I don't know what to think."

His hands tightened on the arms of the navigator's chair. I'd sent everyone from the bridge except the helmsman. "Let me ask you something, Commander. Is it possible to smell lies? Can you do such a thing?"

I had to think about the question for a moment. I'd been ferociously angry, yet I had noticed a different odor when the Krenion had deliberately lied. It was a tinge of something sharp and sour, but I hadn't identified it. "I did smell something off, sir, but I didn't know what it was. Renata has been shifting for many years, so it's safe to assume she could identify the scent of a lie quite easily."

He gave me a nod of agreement and sighed heavily. "I don't know if that evidence will hold any weight with the rest of the Council, but I believe her."

As we approached Ximera, my ship jerked forward, throwing the First to the floor. Alarms blared as the helmsman struggled to right the vessel, slapping switches to cut power.

"We've been caught in the planetary tractor beams, sir! Shall I open a channel to the port?"

I helped the old male to his feet and back to his seat, assisting him with the safety harness. "Yes. Get me Port Commander Denkar."

"Yes, sir." With a few taps on the ship's comm, the grizzled face of one of my oldest friends appeared on the vidscreen.

"Care to tell me what's going on, Denkar?"

He met my eyes in silent apology before reading from a tablet. "By order of Councilor Harkon, I am directed to take the battle cruiser belonging to Warlord Rakon and its crew into custody on suspicion of kidnapping the first councilor. As a dangerous alien megafauna, War Mate Renata Andreyev is to be remanded to the custody of the medical unit in sector four for examination and study."

"Do I look kidnapped?" Fengar asked, his tone acid with contempt.

"No, sir. You look quite healthy to me." He smiled faintly. "I'm just passing along the message and following orders."

"Good. You get to follow my orders now. Get me that mental defective Harkon..." He stopped and took a breath. "Never mind. Haul us in, and make sure you let Harkon know we're arriving. I also want a full contingent of port guards."

"May I ask why, sir?"

"Yes. I plan to arrest the old fool for treason and for colluding with Krenions to abduct War Mate Renata as well as four additional missing shifter females."

"What? Do you mean to tell me—"

"Denkar," I interrupted, "I want you to send a few men to Harkon's chambers if you can do so without him noticing. Guard his office like it contains your fondest wish."

"Harkon's head mounted on the prow of your battle cruiser?" He scowled thunderously and his hand twitched to the blaster on his hip.

There was a reason Denkar and I got along so well. I knew he'd adore Renata. My tiger thought he'd had a most suitable idea, as well. "Close. His office will probably contain the evidence that will let me put it there legally."

"Consider it done. And may I be the first to welcome you and War Mate Renata to Ximera, sir."

I grinned suddenly. Everything was going to turn out. "Thanks. And don't make plans for the next equinox. You're going to be standing with me at my joining."

He chuckled and said, "Wouldn't miss it for the world."

CHAPTER
ELEVEN

RENATA

I shifted, regaining my human form after the door shut behind Rakon. He'd been thoughtful enough to leave my clothes by the door, and sensitive enough to leave me alone. I could hardly fathom being so lucky to have such a considerate male for my own. When I finished dressing, I walked to the lake and hunkered down in the shade of a large tree to think.

Rakon had given me a small comm and I clicked on the record feature to make sense of my thoughts. "Find out what's in sector four. Why did Harkon want to send me there when the prison sector nineteen would have been more logical?"

I'd already deduced the purpose of nineteen from conversation, but the others remained a mystery. Sector two might be a resort or some sort of enclave for the wealthy, but I knew nothing of substance about any of them. I'd planned to research the system before my arrival so I didn't look like a complete idiot in front of my new mate, but I hadn't had the opportunity.

"Find out if Harkon was working for Norkad or if it was the other way around, or if there's another individual involved. Find out where Daiyu, Soledad, and her sisters are. The Krenion mentioned another crew. Find them for questioning. Maybe the brother is a smarter male."

I looked down at the screen on the comm, wondering if there was anything else to add to my list of questions. I couldn't think of anything, but Rakon might have some ideas.

"I wish I knew what was in sector four."

"Is that a formal question, War Mate Renata?" The computer's digitized voice startled me, and I nearly dropped the comm, wondering when I'd get used to having access to so much knowledge when I asked the right questions.

Catching the device before it hit the ground, I said, "Yes. What is in sector four?"

"Sector four of the galaxy containing Ximera 8 and associated colonies was established approximately..."

As usual, the computer irritated me. It was like listening to Sendra when she waxed poetic about historical facts. "Is it a residential sector or does some work or enterprise happen there? What is the purpose of sector four?"

"Sector four contains numerous medical facilities, universities, and research labs dedicated to public health and education. It contains research and preservation complexes for alien flora and fauna that are dangerous or might cause harm to the Ximeran ecosystem."

Ouch. I'd never had much of an ego, but that hurt. I was dangerous alien fauna now? I supposed it was true, even though it was incredibly insulting. My tiger didn't think much of the description either.

"What is the purpose of sector seventeen?" I'd heard that one tossed about as well.

"Sector seventeen is a neutral zone, containing large numbers of known smugglers and contraband. It is also host to various mercenary groups from other systems and is widely considered to be similar to the nineteenth-century American western states in nature."

I didn't know what that meant. I opened my mouth to ask, but the ship made a sudden jerk and sent me flying into a rock, bruising my ribs painfully. For all that the objects in the holo were simulations, they were still solid mass. I scrabbled for the comm I'd dropped and hauled myself to my feet clutching my ribs.

"What happened?" I demanded.

"The Ximeran port commander has locked this vessel into a tractor beam to draw it to the station."

"Why?"

"I do not have that information, War Mate Renata. Give me a moment and I will—"

I ignored the computer and raced from the holo. Several crew members were picking themselves off the deck and milled about in confusion. I pushed through, desperate to reach the bridge and our mate.

I screeched in frustration when the lift panel refused to respond to my touch. Rakon had obviously forgotten to grant me access to the rest of the ship. Again. A large hand reached over my shoulder, slapping the panel with a stiff palm.

Patrek scowled and pushed me into the lift ahead of him. "Computer, grant complete access to War Mate Renata, effective immediately."

"Yes, sir. Your order has been completed."

I heaved out a sigh of relief. It was unconscionable that I hadn't demanded free rein of the ship when I'd arrived. "Thank you. Do you know what's going on?"

"We're being arrested for kidnapping First Councilor Fengar."

I barked out a laugh. "What? Who said that?"

"Harkon, of course."

The door opened and I rushed to my mate, flinging my arms around his waist as I inhaled his scent. My tiger relaxed into his warmth and I realized how much we'd missed him. He dropped an absentminded kiss on my forehead and turned me to face the vidscreen.

"Port Commander Denkar, I present my thoroughly violent and crazed War Mate, Renata Andreyev." He kissed my cheek and grinned. "As you can see, she's quite uncontrollable and slavers and drools everywhere."

I rolled my eyes when Fengar laughed. "Yes, yes, I eat six small adults every day for breakfast. I'm utterly feral."

Chuckling, Rakon picked me up off my feet and settled into his chair with me on his lap. "This is Denkar, *penaka*. We grew up together and he's one of my closest friends."

I nodded respectfully to the older male. Strength shone in his vivid green eyes despite his grizzled beard. "I'm pleased to meet you, Port Commander."

"Denkar, please, War Mate."

"Thank you." I turned in Rakon's lap to face forward. "I assume Councilor Harkon has ordered our arrest?"

"Yes, War Mate."

"What was discussed before I arrived?"

"Harkon has accused you and Rakon of kidnapping me. He will most assuredly be waiting at the dock to take you into custody," Fengar said.

"War Mate, he's also ordered you to be placed into immediate stasis for transport to sector four," Denkar added.

I nodded absently, my brain working furiously. My tiger produced images of two groups facing each other with weapons. She wasn't prescient but knew how to plan a fight. She sought vulnerabilities, tactical advantage and weakness, and was very good at attacking those weak spots.

"Fengar, you can't leave this ship. Harkon's going to try to kill you when you leave."

"I know, child." He smiled wryly and patted my shoulder. "I will get caught in the crossfire and you and Rakon will be blamed." He grinned like a cub caught stealing a treat as he opened the front of his robe to reveal black armor and a blaster strapped to his hip. "Harkon never seems to remember that I used to be a Warlord and commander of my own battle cruiser before his mother had the bad sense to give birth to him."

I blinked at him and my mouth fell open in surprise. With a happy squeal, I leaned over and kissed his bristly cheek, ignoring Rakon's jealous growl. "You are the most duplicitous old male I've ever had the pleasure of meeting, Fen." I kissed him once more and settled back against my mate.

He looked thoughtful for a moment, then grinned. "Fen. I like it, I think. I've never had a nickname before."

The ship vibrated once as the tractor beam pulled us into a docking bay and we fell silent.

In the vidscreen, Denkar touched his hand to his chest and bowed. "I have to go meet Harkon now, but I've already sent a crew to his chambers to ensure your evidence is left intact. I also have a dozen guards standing by. Harkon thinks they are to assist in your capture, but they are aware of the situation and have orders to protect the first councilor."

The vidscreen went dark and we took turns using the lift to the lower levels. I wanted to keep Fengar back so we were able to protect him, but he wasn't having it.

Hip checking me, he strolled into the lift with Patrek, grinning as the door closed.

I rubbed my sore hip and growled as Rakon squeezed my hand. "Don't worry. Harkon will want plenty of witnesses for what he plans. The First is safe enough until we leave the ship."

When we reached the loading dock, we found the doors already open. I hissed in anger as I saw Harkon gesture imperiously toward us. His men already surrounded Fengar and one had put wrist restraints on Patrek.

Through the open bay door, I saw Rakon's friend Denkar standing helplessly under the watchful eyes of more guards. This was not how things were supposed to happen! I watched in horror as dark stripes formed on Rakon's cheeks.

"Don't let your tiger out, Rakon! Harkon will say you attacked and use the excuse to kill you."

"I'm trying..." With visible effort, the stripes receded, and I let out a relieved breath as men restrained him. My tiger wanted to kill them for laying a hand on our mate. Thankfully, she kept herself in check. Shifting would be very bad right now.

Males approached us, one carrying a long stick and a metal collar. I knew those things were for me, but I didn't know the purpose of the stick object.

Fengar's angry shout rang through the bay. "If you lay a hand on the War Mate, I will have you up on so many charges that you won't ever see the light of day in nineteen, boy!"

Harkon smirked. "The old male is clearly senile. Carry out your orders!"

"I'll show you senile, you damned fool!"

I heard a metallic whine emanate from the stick. The sound wasn't loud, but the pitch was so high and so wrong that it hurt. I covered my ears, gritting my teeth at the pain. The man holding the stick pushed it forward as the sound became inaudible.

He brushed the stick across my arm, and I dropped to the floor as unimaginable pain rushed through every cell of my body. The agony was a living thing and stole my breath, my sight, and my self-will. My tiger whimpered once just before another touch from the device forced us into an unwilling, involuntary shift.

Rakon roared, but the sound came from a distance as more men restrained him. I only had enough presence of mind to pray that he didn't shift.

We trembled on the floor, unable to move as the metal collar was snapped around our neck. We watched Fengar gesticulate wildly at Harkon, but the male didn't appear to take any notice as he smirked at us from across the room.

RAKON

The actions of my own people sickened me. I had to watch helplessly as my mate twitched on the floor, the current from the shock stick taking away her control and rendering her helpless. She wouldn't be able to move for at least several minutes. For a human or Ximeran, that time might be measured in hours. Or it might have killed her.

"In what universe is it acceptable to use a shock stick on a female, Captain?" I snarled, though my tiger cautioned calm. Shifting to kill everyone in my hold would do no one any good and would only result in both of us dying.

In his defense, the male looked sick and disgusted by what he'd been ordered to do. "We have to carry out the orders of Councilor Harkon in the first councilor's absence, Commander."

"Except that the first councilor is standing right there, and he isn't happy." I pointed at Fengar, who had Harkon backed into a corner, his blistering curses filling the air. He turned to shout at the men guarding the bay door and they reluctantly moved aside to allow Denkar and his men to pass.

"Councilor Harkon, in standing with Council order 1723.27, you are placed under arrest for high treason!" Denkar's shout rang through the space as he announced his order through the amplifier in his comm.

"I'll have your bars for this, Denkar!" Harkon backed away and lifted a blaster in his shaking hand. "You have no evidence—"

"On the contrary, sir. Your personal terminal contains records of large financial transactions that coincide with the removal of five missing Earth females. Further, you have had direct contact with a known dissident and terrorist, Norkad of sector seventeen, who owns the transport known to have entered the Earth system on the day Soledad Martinez and her sisters were taken."

"Fools!" The blaster turned in Fengar's direction and I heard it power up. "Those animals are going to ruin us! It was fine when the females were just ordinary humans, but this cannot be allowed to pass."

He gestured at my face, and I knew our stripes were visible. "One has already turned a branded Warlord! Do you not see what they're doing to us?"

"Harkon, put down the blaster," Fengar said softly. "It's over now."

He sneered as he faced the first councilor. "And you, old male? You were supposed to be dead so I could take your place!" He raised the blaster and put a thumb on the trigger. "I guess I won't be taking your place, but I'm going to make sure you're dead."

The muzzle glowed brightly and Fengar stepped back as he pulled his own blaster from its holster. He didn't have time! We watched helplessly as the blaster prepared for discharge. Even with armor, a direct shot would likely kill the old man and he knew it. Maybe he would have time to get a shot off, but it wouldn't save his life.

I caught a flash of black-and-white stripes as Harkon's weapon discharged. Her angry roar ringing in my ears, Renata leaped between Harkon and the first councilor, catching the blast in her massive chest. The deck plate shuddered as she fell to the floor, still and unmoving.

"No!" My tiger roared in rage and pain as we sent people flying in our dash toward our dying mate's side. She'd given up her life for someone else. Someone she'd barely known. "No," I whispered, burying my face into the scruff of warm fur at her throat.

I barely saw Fengar strike Harkon in the head with the butt of his blaster, dropping the former councilor to the deck. His words were a low muttering in my head as I cried into our mate's fur. I wanted to take her scent so deeply into our lungs we'd never forget it.

"Restrain him with shock restraints like he used on the War Mate. Nothing will be said if something... untoward should happen to him while he enjoys confinement before his trial," Fengar ordered.

I heard other words but ignored them. How could we live without her? She was the better part of our soul, and we'd had so little time. The room was quiet, and I ignored the guards trickling away.

I felt a hand touch my shoulder. "I can't tell you how sorry—"

"Then don't. Just leave us with our mate." I shrugged away Fengar's gentle touch. It wasn't fair of me, but I couldn't help blaming him. I heard him sigh as he backed away. It was good they all kept their distance.

"Don't leave me, Renata! I never got a chance to tell you that I love you." I lowered my head and let the tears fall into her fur.

We needed time to grieve our mate, and we needed to be left alone with her. Yet as I stretched out beside her, pulling her warm body into my arms, I heard something; a tiny wheezing breath from our mate's mouth. I sat up and put my head to her chest.

"Get a medical team to this location now! War Mate Renata is alive!" Males rushed forward, pushing me out of the way as they surrounded our mate. They had apparently been waiting in case Fengar was injured, but I wouldn't begrudge their presence even though my tiger wanted to start chewing off hands for their overly familiar touch on Renata's fur.

"Heartbeat's weak, but steady. Pulse is faint, respiration labored." The lead medic, his white insignia denoting his battle experience, barked orders at his team and soon they had her carefully moved to a hover board for the trip to the medical wing.

"Do you wish to accompany her, Commander?" He wiped a hand over his face. "We need time to figure out how to treat her in this form, but if she managed to survive a blaster hit, I think she has a good chance of pulling through. If nothing else, she's too damned big for a blaster to do much damage."

"You will speak of her with respect, medic," I growled. "She's the perfect size."

He smiled faintly. "As you say, sir."

Patrek rushed forward, holding out a tablet. "I got this from my lab. It's all the data I managed to pull from old Earth databases on known shifter species. I just did an information dump, so I don't know if anything will help."

The medic took it gratefully. "Thank you. I'm sure we'll find something, sir."

RENATA

We lay on something solid as we moved through unfamiliar corridors. Fuck, everything hurt. Even our claws hurt. It was agonizing to open our eyes so we kept them closed as we moved. The lights were too bright and the stench of unfamiliar males assaulted our sensitive nose. Our belly roiled uncomfortably and we wondered if they were good to eat.

"Renata, please wake up. I know you're in there, *penaka*." Our ears pricked at the sound of our mate's soft voice and we relaxed, knowing he was close enough to protect us until we could shift and heal. We felt his fingers bury themselves into the scruff at our throat and purred brokenly. His low growl of approval washed over us. It had been enough of a response to please him.

"What is that sound?" a voice asked. "It's... amazing."

"She's purring."

"It says in Science Officer Patrek's notes that tigers do not purr."

"They do when they're happy and safe. Be sure she stays that way."

We wanted to chuff laughter at Rakon's angry growl and the medic's squeak of terror, but it was too much effort and even the thought of doing much more than a low purr was too painful. We felt a sharp prick in our foreleg and drifted to sleep with the sound of our mate's rumbling voice in our ears.

We had no idea of the passage of time, but when we woke again, the lights were dimmed, and we heard Rakon snoring next to us.

He'd lain down with us, his arms wrapped around our abdomen and his fingers buried in our belly fur as if he clutched us in sleep.

Our wounds were still painful and we knew the touch from that stick thing affected our muscle control. We hadn't tried to shift, but it would be the best thing. If we could change shape a few times, it would do much toward healing the damage.

The tiger helped as much as she was able, but I hadn't had such a painful shift since I was a cub. I heard a gasp and the low chime of an alarm and felt Rakon stiffen behind me. It seemed to take an agonizing forever, but eventually, I managed to regain my human form.

"Ouch," I slurred. "That's gonna leave a mark." I didn't even have the energy to eat and shivered in Rakon's arms. Even that small movement hurt, but I felt the damage fading away with the last of the effects from the stick. Unfamiliar males crowded close, but Rakon's angry hiss drove them back after someone covered me with a warm blanket.

"How are you feeling, *penaka*?"

"Like I got run over by a transport. Is Fengar okay?"

"He's fine." I felt his chest vibrate with laughter. "Well, if you count furious beyond all known record fine, he's perfectly well."

"Good. I'm glad."

"He's been to visit you several times over the last few days. You are currently the only being on Ximera 8 who he is not yelling at."

"I didn't mean to upset him."

"You didn't. Be thankful you aren't on the Council, though."

I yawned widely. Exhaustion from my shift rode me hard. "Why?"

"Because if I can't trust one, then all are suspect, little tiger. They are all under investigation for suspicion of collusion with Harkon. By the way, you're taking his place on the Council." Robes sweeping around his aged body, Fengar strode into the room and kissed my cheek.

"Too tired, Fen. Talk to me about it tomorrow, but I'll probably say no." I ignored his blustering arguments and drifted off to sleep, safe in our mate's arms. Rakon's delicious scent enveloped me, and I wanted to drown myself in it. Even though I knew I was in no shape for sex, my belly clenched with want and I let out a soft whimper.

Rakon growled, the vibration sending a welcome shiver down my spine. "Behave, mate. You're in no shape for me to fuck you."

"I can't help it," I whispered. His magnificent cock poked into my backside and I felt a trickle of moisture dampen my core. He was right. My body ached and I was so damned tired I couldn't see straight.

But I was content. And safe.

FIVE DAYS later I was deemed well enough to move from medical into our new quarters in the Council building. Fengar was determined to have me on the Council, but I hadn't made a decision yet. I wasn't completely cured, but I could get around on my own and take care of my personal needs without help. Disappointingly, I wasn't well enough for energetic romps with my mate. Instead, we shared soft kisses and learned each other's bodies as we made gentle love to each other.

The suite was gorgeous. Expansive windows on one wall let me see the view from the penthouse. I'd hated using the lift to get up there, but once I saw the ocean from my own quarters, I no longer cared. Ximera was green. Not sickly yellow green of the algae that grew on the surface of most of the free water on Earth, but a vibrant, sundrenched shade I'd never seen before. The Council building was the tallest structure in the city. Rakon told me that nearly all the residents grew their own produce and I liked looking at the rooftop gardens from my window.

I couldn't even imagine such a thing as being able to grow real food, but it was commonplace here. The rumors had been true; Ximera was a place of ease and plenty. Despite Rakon's complaints about the insects and one rather confused bird, I left the windows open to the fresh, unspoiled air. I hadn't even realized Earth was quite so polluted and foul until I smelled the clean breeze from the ocean.

Not all was well on Ximera though. The whole situation was sad and disheartening. Three other members of the Ximeran Council had been found with evidence tying them to the renegade Norkad. Harkon had subverted fully a quarter of the Council, and Fengar had decided to replace the whole lot of them. I heard arguments in the streets and from the lower floors as Ximerans jostled for power in the vacuum Fengar had left.

Part of me wanted to accept the position and try to advocate for my people. Yet a larger part simply wanted to go to our mate's den and do nothing more than hunt and make cubs. I knew the second wish was unrealistic. Rakon had his own work, and I knew that no one else was so uniquely suited to making sure my people were treated fairly, be they human or shifter.

I'd met a few of the human women who had been transported during the early days of the exodus two years prior. They all appeared happy with their new mates, and they glowed with health and good nutrition. One blonde woman named Amy even brought her toddler daughter to our visit. Melissa had been the first cub born on Ximera, though there were a few others now.

No one on Earth or Ximera had seen a cub in years and I couldn't help a few happy tears as the little girl crawled in my lap and tugged on my hair. I cuddled her close as she counted the black streaks in my hair, and laughed when she skipped five. Melissa didn't like five. I smelled the sweet scent of slightly dirty young human and let her trace the stripes I'd allowed to paint my face for her amusement.

Guards shadowed Amy's steps, their stern faces watchful as they tracked little Melissa's movements. No one was taking any chances with the new cubs or their mothers, even though Harkon's plot had been directed at the shifter females.

Child, not cub, I corrected myself. Humans had children.

"Do you mind the guards, Amy?" I had them too, despite being the last person that should need a guard. The building was secure, and I was more than capable of defending myself. But their presence made Rakon and Fengar happy, so I would bear it until they became inconvenient.

"Sometimes." She settled back in her chair as Melissa returned to her lap, her eyes heavy as she cuddled her mother. "I sometimes wish I could go to the bathroom without a babysitter, but I know it's for the best right now." She brightened and gave me a wan smile. "It won't be forever, right?"

I didn't know the answer to that question. Her face fell when I didn't immediately reply. "I don't think it will be forever, but I don't know if or when we'll be completely safe here."

Our visit was cut thankfully short when Melissa started to whimper and Amy took her away for a nap. Her disappointment had been palpable, and I didn't have the words to soothe her.

When the door shut behind her, I walked to the window, inhaling deeply. I hoped that Rakon would return soon. He'd promised me a trip to the beach today and I was more than ready to go outside. There was room enough in the suite to shift, but I could only pace in an enclosed room for so long before the action became maddening.

The door chimed and I turned to smile at my mate, but blinked in surprise when he was followed by Denkar. Rakon hadn't allowed other males into our suite before and I wondered what was wrong.

Rakon shot me a blinding smile of pure joy as he swung me up into his arms. "We have a surprise for you, War Mate."

"What?" I struggled to get down, but he kissed me so thoroughly I forgot what I was doing. My core grew wet with want as I purred for my mate. Though I'd asked many times, Rakon refused to give me the lively sex I wanted until he was sure I was healed. When Denkar cleared his throat and laughed, he finally set me on my feet.

"We have a Kodiak bear in the space dock. She's thin and a little sickly from malnutrition, but alive and safely in stasis. I thought you would want to be the first to welcome her."

I put a hand on my heart and Rakon's strong arms held me up when I would have collapsed. "Where did you find her?"

"She was found injured and unconscious in the Bering Sea by a scout vessel only a few days after you were taken, but we don't know what happened to her. Her genetics match yours, *penaka*." He swung me around again, his joy infectious. "The crew put her in stasis to keep her safe for the trip."

"Keep them safe, you mean," Denkar added.

"That too. Would you like to see her?" Rakon asked.

"Yes, but we're taking her somewhere out in the open when we let her out of stasis. Bears like confinement even less than tigers."

"I know just the place."

CHAPTER
TWELVE

RAKON

The place I had in mind for the bear's release was only a few hours outside the city. It was far enough away from population centers that she would have room to roam if she decided to stay, yet close enough we could watch her. I told myself it was coincidence it was a short distance from the vacation cabin my parents had owned when I was a child. She could use it if she wanted to be human and it would be a safe place for other shifters to acclimate to Ximera.

Renata told me the place wasn't ideal for a Kodiak, but she would find game and adapt quickly. It clearly was ideal for her tiger and stripes raced across her cheeks as she peered out the window of our vehicle. Denkar drove the heavy transport carrying the Kodiak shifter. I wasn't sure why the male wanted to come, but he'd been fascinated by the massive creature, easily twice the size of Renata's tiger.

The choice of location had another benefit. Thousands of Ximeran males demanded to be tested for genetic matches with her and we'd had to lock her stasis chamber under heavy guard to keep her safe. If we'd found a match, we would have allowed the male access, but no match had been discovered thus far.

Denkar broke the seal on the stasis chamber and backed away as Renata and I shifted. We felt the bear would be more comfortable in the presence of other shifters. She stumbled as she climbed from the unit, but soon regained her feet and swung her head back and forth, her nose working furiously. Shaggy brown fur blew in the breeze as she moved. Her rounded ears twitched as she picked up birdsong.

When she spotted us, she lowered her head, her chuffing growls loud in the meadow, before ambling toward the tree line. She passed Denkar, ignoring him, but stopped before taking more than a few steps, her mouth opening wide to draw his scent across her palate.

My mate was shifted and moving forward before I'd had a chance to breathe. "Hold very still, Denkar. She'll chase you if you try to run." She was no match for the bear, and I crouched, preparing myself to defend her.

I didn't need to worry. The bear had eyes only for Denkar. She sat up on her hindquarters, resting her massive front paws on the vehicle and capturing him between her forelegs as she rubbed her head on his chest.

Dropping to her feet, she growled then took his hand into her jaws and tugged to convince him to follow.

"What is she doing?" he asked, his voice tinged with panic.

Renata chuckled. "She's chosen a mate."

"But I didn't submit a sample! I don't even know this woman!"

She arched an eyebrow and smirked. "I don't think she cares." Turning to the bear, she said, "It's impolite to take a Ximeran male without permission. Shift and introduce yourself, Kodiak."

Mist filled the air and I watched as a tall, muscular woman stepped out. Brown hair trailed to her ass, and she glared at us with dark eyes. She was too thin though, and resembled Renata before I'd gotten a few good meals into her. Old battle scars decorated her arms and legs, evidence of her struggle. Some were red and inflamed, but they didn't appear to bother her. Or, like Renata, she ignored their presence in favor of something more important.

"Bossy tigers. Go away while I deal with my mate." Her words were heavily accented, but clear.

Renata growled deep in her throat. "Introduction, Kodiak. And he must agree to the mating before I see a hint of fang."

The bear flinched at Renata's order. Despite her bluster, it was clear she understood the hierarchy of shifter races. Yet she spun around to face my mate with arrogance and something I thought might be fear in her eyes.

"You have a mate, Panteris. Give me mine." She took two steps forward and shifted, her angry roar filling the air.

"Kodiak, you do not want to fuck with me," Renata warned. "Shift back right now."

She strode forward, still in her human form, until she was nose to nose with the bear. Yet her voice was gentle. "Shift and we'll talk. You're in a new place and I can tell you've been injured. When you're calm, you and Denkar can talk and rest."

The bear shifted once more and lowered her human head. "Will there be food that is not the thin, pale ones who attempted to take me? They are not good food, and they have things that hurt."

Renata growled and mist formed around her. She exuded a wave of power that made the bear cry out and drop to her belly in supplication. Hell, it made me want to do the same thing.

I wanted to kill something. How many shifters had they taken from under our noses? And where had they gone? Renata helped the bear to her feet and touched her face as she whispered soothing words of comfort. She leaned forward until their foreheads met. I imagined they shared scents of each other, well-being, and the knowledge that they weren't alone.

"As much as you can eat. And someone will tend your injuries when you allow it." A smaller wave of power emanated from her, making the bear shiver. "And I promise there are no Krenion on this planet."

The bear looked up, a hopeful expression in her huge brown eyes. "There is game here."

"Yes, but you may not take humans or Ximerans. You may also ask for food to be brought to you. Now give me your name."

The bear lowered her head in submission. "Anya Aliyova."

"Welcome to Ximera 8, Anya. The gentleman you're determined to bite is Port Commander Denkar." Her expression hardened and her power washed over us again. "We do not accept forced mating here. He must ask for your bite. Do you understand?"

Anya lowered her head, hunching her shoulders in submission. "Yes, Panteris."

"Good. We're leaving now. Have fun!"

"Wait!" Anya stretched out her hand, catching Renata's arm. "What do I do?"

"Get to know your new mate, hunt, eat, get healthy, and give him a reason to accept you." She stroked the bear's shoulder, offering comfort. "Let him care for you. You're safe."

"Can I reach you if I need something?"

"Denkar will give you a comm and show you how to use it. You'll be fine."

I shifted and reached into the vehicle for the bag we'd packed for her. "Here are some clothes to get you started. Use the comm or ask Denkar if you need anything else."

Her hand shook as she took the bag. "Why are you being so kind, Panterum? I'm only a bear."

I'd heard the honorific on Renata's great-grandmother's vids, but never thought it would be applied to me. "You are a shifter and this is your home now." I waved my hand at the verdant landscape. "You could return to Earth if you want. No one will stop you, but I think you'll like it here. If you decide you can't live among humans or Ximerans, we can relocate you somewhere else where you can live as a bear."

A tear rolled down her cheek and she brushed it away with a

work-roughened hand. "I can never repay your generosity," she whispered.

"All you have to do is welcome any shifters we find and tell us if you know where others might be."

"The wolves and the last two orca calves are hidden in what used to be Wales, Alaska. There are two mated pairs of bears, plus my brothers as well." She wrinkled her nose. "They're eating carrion and any stray humans they find, but there are very few humans left who aren't part of the community. I was hunting for food for them when I was caught and injured."

"Thank you, Anya. We'll pass along the news and hopefully bring them home very soon." I leaned close to take in her scent so I would know her. "And do yourself a favor. Tell Denkar what happened to you. When you're ready, your Panteris will want to know as well."

I helped Renata into the vehicle, and we left them alone. They'd work things out. Denkar wasn't a bear, but he wasn't without the ability to defend himself. The unmated males would probably demand genetic proof, but the deed was done as far as I was concerned.

As we drove away, I watched Denkar take Anya's hand and lead her in the direction of the cottage.

"Tell me about the orca. Are they a fish species?"

She chuckled. "No, I think they're whales."

"What's the difference?"

"They breathe air, but I don't know much about them other than that they were massive carnivores. So much of our knowledge has been lost that Patrek is probably a better source of information about them."

For Renata to call a shifter massive was saying something. "How big?"

"Multiple tons. Sendra told me they were the biggest shifter she knew of, but I really have no idea."

"Fuck." I couldn't even imagine something that size. There were large sea creatures in our oceans, but the largest was perhaps the size of Anya's bear.

She laughed and squeezed my hand. "Don't worry so much. They can shift and walk into a transport just like I did."

I joined her laughter. I wasn't sure why I'd thought we'd have to transport them as orcas. "Are you up for another trip?"

"Sure. What do you have in mind?"

"I want to take you to my, well, our house just outside the city. It's not as luxurious as our quarters in the Council building, but it's right on the beach and has a huge nature preserve behind it."

"Will we live there?"

"Either there or in the Council building. Whichever suits you is fine with me."

"I would rather not live so close to other people, if that's all right. I don't want to insult Fengar, but the thought that people are living on the other side of my walls makes my flesh crawl."

"Mine too. I never liked having too many people close by. Many Ximerans live in multifamily buildings, but it never suited me."

"Good. I was afraid you liked the quarters he gave us."

"If you accept a position on the Council, we will have to stay there sometimes." I didn't want her to not accept just because she hated the apartment, but I wasn't going to mislead her.

She shrugged her thin shoulders. "It's nice enough, but we want a den of our own when we bear cubs."

I loved the thought of her pregnant with my cubs. I couldn't wait to see it. "The house is pretty wrecked. It used to belong to my grandparents and we've been using it for storage for years. I've got a couple of rooms cleaned out, but the rest of it..." I shook my head and tried to smile. "Anyway, try to keep an open mind."

"I'm sure I'll love it."

She would probably hate it, but I had enough wealth that she could do whatever she wanted with the old place. It was structurally sound, but I hadn't done anything with it aside from critical maintenance and it looked like a trash heap. I held no illusions that it would please my mate, but I hoped she appreciated the work I'd done on the bedroom and kitchen.

I spent the drive back to the city telling her about the sights we passed. She was interested in everything and demanded that we stop several times. Other males tried to touch her when we stopped and I was pleased that she could evade them without being rude. The only one she allowed to lay a hand on her was an elder with a crutch leaned up against his bench.

I was jealous, but the sensation was muted by the male's age and infirmity as she perched on his lap and hugged him. My throat tightened when she kissed his cheek and he grinned widely as a tear leaked from his eye.

Eventually, he smirked at me and patted her hip to shoo her away. Despite the presence of several dozen human females on Ximera, they were rarely seen, and none would have approached an elder to give him comfort. Given her past deprivation and hardship, it was unfathomable to me that she maintained such grace and empathy for someone who could be of no benefit to her. The First Councilor had been right to insist that she take a position on the Council. She could do much good for Ximera.

It was late by the time we reached the beach and I stopped at my favorite fish stand to feed her. She'd loved the replicated *mara* my cook had given her while on my battle cruiser. Fresh *mara* was infinitely better.

She peered up at the handwritten menu, biting her lip. "I don't know what to choose."

I blinked in surprise when I realized it was written in English along with standard Ximeran. Yet I was pleased. I liked seeing my people welcome the humans.

The son of the owner grinned and winked at her, but sobered when I growled. "I'll give you a taste of everything, War Mate. You may choose what pleases you."

He handed her a small dish containing a few bites of sautéed *mara* with herbs and the spicy root that went so well with them. My cock hardened when she moaned in pleasure at the first bite of the shellfish.

"Is this *mara*?"

"Yes, but it's fresh. What you had aboard my ship was replicated."

"I definitely want this." She poked at it and took another bite. "What makes it so spicy?"

"It's called *grakon*, War Mate. It's a bulb that grows wild on most of Ximera. In that dish, it's roasted before being added to the *mara*. It softens the flavor and makes it a little bit sweet. You can also spread it on bread."

"Can I have some?"

I let her taste everything, loving her facial expressions as she ate. Some things she didn't like. She hadn't liked the *emba* at all. The sinuous, cartilaginous fish was an acquired taste. We eventually got a large meal of her favorites and toted the food down to the beach.

We sat in the sand and ate as the twin moons rose in the sky. She was quiet and only responded to direct questions as she ate her meal.

"Want to talk about it?" The question was a variation on the "we need to talk" speech, but something bothered my mate and I was desperate to fix it.

"I'm just..." She paused and drew her knees to her chest. "Happy, I think. But I keep wondering when this will end and something bad will happen, you know?"

I didn't know, but we'd lived wildly different lives. I'd matured in relative safety while she'd been fighting for every meal and struggling to survive. "Maybe it's time to relax and enjoy what you've got."

"I'm not sure I can. Norkad is still out there, still hunting shifters. How can I rest in comfort while they're in danger?"

"Get up. It's time to go home." I pulled her up from the sand and we collected our trash. It was time to soothe our mate, and we knew just the way to do it. She stiffened when I slapped her ass to get her moving, but I knew she wouldn't react with violence.

I didn't know what it meant to be Panterum, but I'd figure it out. She would bow to our wishes and submit. And then we could make her happy.

RENATA

Rakon helped me back into his vehicle for the short trip to his house. I couldn't wait to see our new den even though I knew he was nervous about showing it to me. He didn't understand that the condition of his house didn't matter. The only thing that did matter was that it was ours and would be the place we'd raise our cubs.

A den didn't have to be luxurious or fancy; it had to be comfortable and safe.

The house was quite different from the other dwellings I'd seen on Ximera and looked very old. Whole trees had been used to construct the walls, and the foliage dripping from the rooftop garden added whimsy to the solid structure. The path leading to the front stairs was made of smoothly laid stone, seamless under my feet and worn in places from the tread of many people before me. I loved it immediately.

I loved it because it blended with the contrasting environments of beach and forest. I loved the overgrown foliage that would make excellent hiding places for enterprising cubs. I loved the huge windows overlooking the sea. He took my hand and led me around to the back of the house.

A large pond took up most of the space and I saw fish playing under the surface of the clear water, their red and gold bodies flashing in the waning sunlight. A stone fire pit stood off to one side, surrounded by comfortable chairs covered by a wooden structure overgrown with flowering vines, their scent perfuming the air. The pond was the perfect size for young cubs to learn to swim before they braved the sea.

I hoped the fish weren't too expensive. My claws twitched and I knew it would be impossible to keep cubs from eating them when their mother could barely control her desire to wade in and start fishing. Despite having a full belly, we still wanted to gobble one down. My face got hot when Rakon chuckled and touched my shoulder to draw my attention away from the little treats.

"Ready to see the inside?"

"Of course! This is amazing!"

He took my hand, then led me through a heavy glass door. When we walked in, I understood his trepidation. The house was littered with, well, objects. We had to wind our way through the mass of furniture, boxes, and other debris. Where had all these things come from?

"I'm so sorry, Renata. I know it looks bad."

"There are so many things!"

He sighed and led me into the only clean room in the house and helped me sit at the kitchen table. "The house used to belong to my mother's family, and we've used it for storage for years. I never had the opportunity to clean it out. I've only done this kitchen and the master suite."

I tried to look beyond the clutter to see the bones of the house and realized it would be perfect once we got the mess cleared. "It will be wonderful when we've gotten it cleaned up. Will you be upset to see your things stored elsewhere?"

"I don't remember where half this stuff came from." He scrubbed a hand through his hair and scowled as he gazed at the mess in the other rooms.

I laughed and said, "I'm sure we can find something to do with it." Leaning over to kiss his cheek, I added, "It's fine, really. We can clean up and save the things that fit in the space. I'm sure it won't take very long."

"I should just have everything hauled outside and set fire to it."

"No! There are some nice things!" I pointed out one chair that had caught my eye. It was almost as wide as a small sofa and would be perfect to cuddle my cubs while I read to them. "I love that green chair over in the corner."

A wistful smile stole across his face. "That was my mother's favorite chair. She'd sit sideways with her legs hanging off the end while she read or watched the vids." He frowned suddenly as he searched the room. "But I don't see the table that went with it."

What a beautiful memory. I was sure there were others he would associate with something in that pile of objects, but he was right. We'd have to go through everything and dispose of the vast majority. "I love the outside. This is the perfect place to den, and I'm sure we'll find the table you mentioned."

"It's a mess. You don't have to say things just to be kind."

"Hadn't you heard?" I grinned and allowed my fangs and claws to erupt. "I'm feral and a dangerous alien fauna. I don't do kind. You'll see that if you try to throw away that chair."

He burst into the laughter I'd wanted to hear. "I'll show you dangerous, mate of mine." He growled and lifted me out of my chair, and I squealed when he tossed me over his shoulder. When I struggled, he swatted my backside, the sting rendering me speechless.

"What was that for?"

"For being so perfect I can't resist you." His purposeful footsteps took us into another room, and I gasped at the sight.

This room was my vision for the rest of the house. One wall was glass, looking over the beach, with a door set into the windows leading out to a patio with a seating area and a freestanding fireplace. Steam rose from a circular tub in a corner.

The other walls were painted in swirling shades of gray and blue, reminiscent of the sea, and recessed illumination gave the space a warm glow. A massive vidscreen took up most of the wall opposite the bed. The wooden floors were bare of coverings, but several thick rugs decorated the space surrounding a cozy sitting area near a stone fireplace.

I saw a glimpse of a sumptuous bathroom through a door, but I ignored it for the moment.

I'd lost my train of thought at the sight of that bed. It was big enough that both of us could be in our tiger forms and still have room to spare. Carved posts jutted up from each corner, nearly reaching the ceiling. The head and foot had large panels decorated with more carvings. White linen billowed in the breeze from the open window. It looked like something from a decadent fantasy.

"Do you like it? When I learned I'd been granted you, I had it copied from an image I saw of a home in the British colonies in the Caribbean. I wasn't sure how it would turn out, but I think the artist did a good job. I wanted to give you something beautiful from Earth."

"I—"

He coughed uncomfortably and set me on my feet. "I'm sorry. We can get rid of—"

I purred, the sound drowning out the calls of birds and insects from outside as I shoved him backward until he fell on that wonderful, gorgeous bed. He'd had it made for me. Just because he wanted me to remember something beautiful from my home planet. Just because he wanted me to be happy.

I straddled his waist, my hands settled on his hard chest. His muscles twitched under my fingers, and I wanted to dig my claws into his delicious flesh. I leaned down and trailed kisses over his throat, relishing his gasps of pleasure when I nipped him.

"I love this room. I love this amazing bed. I love this house." I scooted up until I could reach his mouth and kissed him, biting his lip until I tasted his sweet blood as it trickled over my tongue. "And I love you."

I nuzzled my face into the crook of his neck and licked at the scar decorating his shoulder. My scar. My mark that told the whole universe he was mine. He growled and his hands tightened on my hips.

He rolled me over and I squeaked in surprise when he settled himself between my thighs. "Mine," he whispered, his broken purr sounding low in my ears. He tore away my clothes with bared claws, leaving not a shred of fabric to cover me. I wanted to protest, but his pupils elongated and narrowed as his eyes flashed amber. He opened his mouth and his fangs dropped low, glinting white in the setting sun.

Now was not the time to do anything but obey. When he moved backward to lift my sex to his mouth, I decided I would walk naked back to our quarters in the Council building if I could guarantee he wouldn't stop that delicious thing he did with his tongue.

His mobile, searching tongue was rough like his tiger's as he devoured me and his feral, satisfied growl made me shudder as he licked my folds.

"I love the way you smell," he growled as he rubbed his face into my pussy. "I want to bottle this scent so I have it all the time."

Oh. Fuck. Rakon had once told me he got it wrong every time we talked. Yet when he said things like that... "God! Rakon!" I grabbed his hair and pushed his face into my pussy, desperate for more contact with that amazing tongue he used with such wild abandon.

"Bad girl!" His strong hands flipped me over so I lay on my belly and he slapped my ass. "You will take what I give you."

We both knew I could escape the ropes he used to tie my hands over my head. And we both knew I was strong enough to prevent the pillows shoved under me that lifted my hips up. We both knew that the Panterum's mate would do as she was told.

"So beautiful." His hands stroked my spine and I whimpered softly, desperate for a firmer touch. His hand fell to my ass once more, delivering the pain he demanded of me. It was all I needed. The sting sent heat straight to my needy clit and I gasped in pleasure as his hand continued to fall on my unprotected flesh raised up for his pleasure.

My logical human mind wanted to escape, wanted to equate the harsh blows with the abuse we'd suffered at Norkad's hands. The feral part of me, not tiger, but wild, reveled in our mate's attention.

My ass grew hot and Rakon stopped, stroking me with his warm palm.

His fangs pricked my backside and I let out a tortured moan as the sharp teeth raked my sensitive flesh. "You're so fucking wet. Do you like being tied and spanked?"

I shook my head and cried out when he laid another stinging blow across my ass. "Please, Rakon..."

"Please what, sweet tiger?" His hand trailed upward, and I gasped as his thumb pressed against my asshole. I felt him shift behind me and something bigger and much harder than his finger prodded against the tender opening.

"P-please..." I hated myself for those needy moans, but Rakon had me undone. I whined and purred low in my throat to soothe him, to no avail. His hand met the tender flesh of my thigh, and I couldn't help my screech of pain and pleasure.

"Words, Renata. I need your words." He lowered himself until I felt his hard body against my back and his teeth against the flat of my shoulder. His teeth scraped against my tender skin. "I'm going to be in your ass very soon, little mate, but not today."

Fuck. I had no idea what to say to that. His thumb twitched and breached the tight ring at the entrance of my asshole, and I stiffened at the uncomfortable sensation.

My ass tightened on the intrusion.

"Relax and push out," he whispered. Another slap on my ass made me do as I'd been told, and he pressed another finger inside me, touching nerves I'd never known I had. It seemed odd to me that such a thing would be pleasurable, but I trusted that my mate wouldn't hurt me.

With his free hand, he pinched my clit as he scissored his fingers inside me. I'd thought the dark intrusion would hurt, and despite his dirty words and spanks to my ass, his fingers moved slowly as he gave me time to adjust. My hands clenched on the soft rope he'd used to tie me to the bedposts as I tried to catch my breath enough to speak.

"Fuck! I'm going to…" I whimpered in disappointment when he pulled his fingers away from my body.

"You aren't coming until I say so," he ordered, his voice rough. I heard the need in the low rumbles emanating from his chest.

"Rakon, please!" I couldn't help the whine in my voice and lowered my head to the soft sheets as tears of frustration pricked at my eyes.

He chuckled darkly and tugged my hips up. His hard cock rubbed against my pussy, and I shivered when he slipped inside me, stretching me almost painfully. "Push your thighs together, *penaka*."

Once he'd helped me reposition my thighs, I groaned as he eased himself inside me once more. The new position made me so damned tight, I felt every vein and ridge on his thick cock. I felt the brush of hair roughened thighs on my tender skin as he leaned forward and nibbled at my shoulder.

"I want to bite you there, little mate. I want to leave a mark on you so everyone knows who you belong to."

His hot breath wafted past my ear, blowing a strand of hair into my face as I panted in need. "Please, Rakon…"

He sat up and pulled out, leaving me bereft. I cried out in desperation, and he slapped my ass once more.

"Patience, love. I don't want this over too soon."

He flipped me to my back and drew a bared claw down the middle of my chest. His touch was gentle and didn't break the skin, but the teasing scratch made me shiver. I nearly shot up off the bed when he grinned wickedly and tapped my clit with that sharp claw. His large hand pressed into my belly held me still for his greedy fingers.

The claw disappeared and he thrust two fingers into my pussy, curling them up to stroke the roughened flesh inside. I screamed at the firm touch and my vision went black at the overwhelming sensation. Dark pleasure rose up and I held my breath as I tried to hold my orgasm at bay.

I knew he wouldn't let me come so soon, but I hissed when he pulled his dripping fingers from my pussy. "Stop teasing me!"

I hated the whine in my voice, but I loved his joyful laughter, especially when I saw his eyes flash amber. His tiger was joining in our play.

"Soon, love. I want to see you mindless first. I want to see you forget your own name." He growled low and nipped my hip, his fangs pressing almost hard enough to break the skin. "But you won't forget mine. I want you to scream my name when I finally let you come."

His hot breath touched my core, and I was lost as his rough tongue licked me from my ass all the way up to my clit. His large hands held my thighs splayed open as he teased me, sucking and nipping at my outer lips as he carefully avoided my clit.

A few tears leaked from my eyes as I tried desperately to lift my hips to meet his teasing mouth. I just needed a little more... Something. I needed... I screamed at the sharp blow he delivered to my splayed pussy. The wet sound made me clench in need, and I whimpered when he rubbed his dripping hand on my belly, coating me with my own juices.

"Uh-uh, bad girl," he chided. "Be still and I'll give you what you need."

I wanted to cry in earnest when he stood up and left me. How was this giving me what I needed? He returned quickly and knelt on the bed next to my head, a piece of black fabric clenched in one fist.

"Relax, *penaka*. I want you to relax and feel."

He laid the cloth over my eyes, lifting my head to secure it in the back. He smoothed my hair, making sure to keep it free of the knot he tied. My tiger paced in anticipation and nervousness, but he soothed her with a soft kiss. I tasted myself on his lips, the scent of my arousal coating my palate.

He swiped his fingers across my wet pussy and touched them to my lips. "Suck," he ordered, his voice rough with desire. "I want you to taste how delicious you are."

Without my sight, the rest of my acute senses grew even sharper. Hearing and scent. Taste. I relaxed as I sucked his wet, sticky fingers into my mouth and relished his groan when I swirled my tongue around them to lick up every bit of the salty sweet flavor of me. My pussy spasmed and I pressed my thighs together as he fed me my own juices. I could come from this alone.

His heart beat faster as he pulled his fingers away from my mouth. I lifted my head to chase after them, but when I opened my mouth, his cock pressed against my lips. I sucked him greedily as his hand clenched the back of my head, holding me still as he thrust shallowly into my mouth.

Drool trickled down the sides of my chin as I tried to fit him inside my mouth. He cursed loudly and his hips shot forward until he was lodged in the back of my throat. I swallowed desperately and he pulled back when I coughed.

"Shit, Renata!" His low growl of pained need made me open my mouth and search for his cock once more. I knew I resembled a blind cub seeking a teat, but I wanted him back in my mouth. Wanted the slow trickle of sweet fluid beading at the head of his cock. It was spicy and delicious, hot with desire, and I wanted it back more than I wanted my next breath.

He left me and I forced myself to be patient. I breathed through my nose, trying to quell the sense of panic but I knew he wouldn't leave me wet and wanting. He would see to my needs in his own good time. I wished it would be soon, though.

He pushed my knees up and I felt a trickle of cold liquid trail down to my exposed asshole. His fingers touched me there again, rubbing the slippery fluid into my crinkled rosebud.

"Relax and breathe out, *penaka*."

I did as he asked and felt a hard object press against my back hole. It wasn't his fingers, and it was too cold to be his cock. I wanted to move away from the intrusion, but we trusted our mate. He wouldn't harm us. I breathed once more and pushed as the object slipped past the ring of muscle and lodged inside me.

"Oh, my good girl," he breathed. He pushed two fingers into my pussy and thumbed my clit, making me clench down on them.

"Oh, fuck!"

He laughed at me, but I had no words for the sensation. I was full, so damned full. The object in my bottom pushed against sensitive nerves and when he put his fingers inside me, it was almost too much. Yet it wasn't enough. I wanted more.

And when the object started to vibrate inside me, I roared.

CHAPTER
THIRTEEN

RAKON

By all the ancient gods, she was perfect. Our mate was everything we hadn't known we'd needed. Her beautiful body was stretched out like an offering, flushed pink as black stripes swirled and disappeared on her hot flesh.

It was all I could do not to spill my cum on her belly. And when she'd sucked me into her mouth, trying desperately to swallow my length down her throat, I'd been undone.

And she was ours.

Her striped hair fanned out under the blindfold, framing her beautiful face. I loved seeing her tied and at my mercy, blinded to my whims. I shook my head and got back to work. If I wasn't careful, I'd come like a boy with his first whore just from looking at her.

Shit! When she'd taken that plug like an accomplished courtesan, I'd had to squeeze the base of my cock hard enough to make my fingers hurt so I didn't come. She would be so tight and the vibrations against my...

"Does it feel good, *penaka*?" I had to separate Renata from the beautiful creature stretched out under me. My mate, but so much more. I had to focus on her pleasure—focus on her body before I lost myself and failed at the task I'd set. I'd promised to make her forget her name and scream mine. I wanted to forget my name and scream hers. Until neither of us knew where one stopped and the other began. Until we were one.

I wanted to erase the memory of our first ignoble coupling when I'd taken her in the dirt against a tree, caring nothing for her pleasure.

I squeezed my cock hard enough that it hurt, but it eventually softened just a little. When I thought I could look at her without spraying cum on her face, I closed my eyes and knelt down to take her hot flesh into my mouth.

I would be fine if I didn't look, right? It didn't help. Her delectable scent overwhelmed me, and I had to squeeze my cock again as I devoured her dripping cunt. I'd always loved edging my past partners. I'd loved seeing them lose all control as they screamed my name. I'd been good at it, too, but none of those females had meant a damned thing to me. I'd used them to bolster my ego.

But they'd served a purpose. They taught me how to pleasure my mate. I sucked gently on her clit as I used two fingers to massage the rough spot in her passage that would give her pleasure. It was a delicate balancing act. Too much pressure in either place would hurt her, but too little would only frustrate my sweet mate.

I focused on her heart rate and breathing, easily heard with my newly increased perception. She cried out and clenched down on my fingers as I sucked at her flesh. The vibrations in her ass must be driving her mad.

"Come for me, *penaka*." I sucked hard on her clit as I curled my fingers against that patch of roughened flesh inside her. She roared as she came, bathing my face with a gush of her sweet slick.

We wanted to roll in the delicious stuff, cover our fur with it until the scent became embedded in our skin. I let the vibe in her ass keep buzzing as I eased her down with gentle flicks of my tongue. I'd be balls deep in her ass soon, but not today.

Cubs first, manslut.

My tiger had a point, but I didn't answer. I was too busy moving our mate to the next pinnacle.

RENATA

I couldn't breathe. I'd forgotten how. I'd never come so hard. The orgasm he'd given me almost hurt, and I shivered with aftershocks. He stroked my pussy and murmured sweet sounds I couldn't understand.

He'd taken my hearing along with my sight. I could only feel and draw his musky scent across my palate, drooling at the smell of our mate. I felt his hands stroke up and down my inner thighs as he spread me wide. The air was cold against my wet pussy as he turned me so I lay on my belly. He centered his beautiful cock against my opening.

I wished I could see him. I wished I could have that magnificent flesh in my mouth again. I was sure I could do better. I would please him.

The vibration from the toy he'd pressed into my ass over-whelmed me and I arched up in offering to his unceasing depreda-tion. I let out a feral sound as he pushed his thick cock into my needy pussy, a mix of growl, purr, and whine. I couldn't believe such a sound was produced by my human throat.

"Fuck, Renata." He grabbed my hair with one hand and wrapped the other around my throat. His heavy balls slapped at my clit as he thrust into me. He didn't choke me, but I would have gladly given up my air for him. His thumbs stroked my windpipe as he kept me still.

He pounded into me, his cock touching the neck of my womb. And I loved it. I loved the hurt, loved the way he owned me, loved the way he took me. The object in my ass vibrated, the toy making me tighter for him as it stimulated those dark nerve endings. Every thrust pushed it deeper inside me and I tilted my hips to accept more of him.

He reached down and pinched my clit. "Come for me, mate."

I clenched down at his growled order, and he swelled inside me. His balls were snug against my pussy and wished I could pet them while he came inside me. Lights unseen lit stars and fire in my eyes and I lost myself in the rapture he gifted me. "Rakon!"

RAKON

She collapsed into a boneless heap, her breaths tearing in her lungs as her heart labored to catch up. I wanted to be smug about that, but my heart raced just as fast. Renata Andreyev officially rocked my universe.

I would never be the same and I loved every minute of it.

I lifted my weight from her prone form, worried that I'd suffocate her. She was so tiny and thin. And she snored.

I loved the sound of her purring breaths. Loved her.

My cock was still half hard when I pulled out, but I ignored it. We were done. She was done. She was less than an Earth week from a debilitating blaster wound. I didn't know why I had to keep reminding myself of that.

If she hadn't been shifted when she jumped in front of that blaster... I shook my head and straightened, propelling myself toward the bathroom. I couldn't think about it. It was too hard to consider how close I'd come to losing her.

I dampened a cloth with warm water and returned to my mate to bathe our exertions from her beautiful body. She snorted and I wanted to laugh. So fucking cute. I tossed the cloth aside and crawled into bed with her, pulling the sheet over our cooling bodies as insects and night birds lent their music to the evening.

Sleep came hard. I wasn't willing to waste a minute of our time to something as useless as rest, but I wasn't able to deny my body's need.

RENATA

"Wake up, Renata."

Rakon's soft voice prodded me from sleep and I swiped out a claw to drive him away. I was warm and comfortable tucked into our nest.

He caught my hand and pressed a kiss to my knuckles. "I have to go. I've been summoned to Council, but you can rest until you're ready to get up."

"M'kay. Get out and let me sleep."

He laughed and I felt bad for not having the energy to go with him. I should be there if I planned to take a Council seat. He kissed me and the door shut behind him as I drifted into a sullen doze.

I floated for a long time in that ephemeral state between lucidity and sleep, but incessant pounding at the door finally roused me from my rest. I growled, my tiger irritated and out of sorts as I searched the closet for something to wear. I kept things simple and tugged a plain dress over my head, then stomped through the mess in the front room to reach the door.

I slammed it open. "What!"

I felt horrible when I saw Anya's lower lip wobble and her eyes fill with tears.

"I'm sorry, Panteris. May I make an appointment?"

"Shit. No, honey." I took her arm and dragged her inside. I was such a bitch. I pulled her into the kitchen and made her sit.

"I'm sorry. I didn't get much sleep last night. Why aren't you with Denkar?"

Her lip wobbled once more and she sniffed. "I—"

"Are you hungry?" I interrupted.

"No, Panteris. I just... He asked me to leave, and I don't know where to go."

"Did you bite him?"

"Yes. He asked, but I shouldn't have."

"Famous last words," I muttered. I searched through the cupboards for food but found only canned crap I could have gotten on Earth. "Are you up to getting furry?"

"Excuse me?"

"I'm going fishing." I gave her a toothy grin. "Rakon tells me there are fish bigger than my tiger in the ocean."

I opened the door and stripped, dropping my dress in a puddle on the floor as I embraced my tiger and raced toward the beach. I felt Anya behind me and grinned.

We reached the water line at the same time and began to swim. I looked for seabirds that would mark schools of fish when I saw the sleek gray of a huge, scaled beast breach the surface several yards out. Rakon had been right. The fish was massive and would feed both of us.

It breached again, its cavernous maw wide as it fanned spiked dorsal fins. Anya darted in, her claws bared to rend its gills. Blood streaked red tendrils across the water and I inhaled the delicious scent as I tended to its other side.

This monster would take both of us to haul to the beach. It thrashed, slapping our head with its massive tail. This was not the fish we'd scooped from Rakon's tank.

This was a predator in its own right, and we would have to pay attention.

We couldn't help the joy welling as we stalked the bleeding fish, herding it toward shore. Anya snarled, her teeth bared as she sank her fangs deeply into the creature just above its gills and dragged it out of the water.

We took the other side and helped her pull the fish up the beach. It fought against us and opened bleeding wounds on us as we struggled. And it was glorious and wonderful. It thrashed as we buried our fangs into its viscera.

And we feasted upon its flesh, gorging ourselves upon the rich meat. We consumed the offering until we were glutted, and the carcass was white bone.

I shifted, my tiger somnolent from the heavy meal, and bent my knee as I lounged against the sand.

"Tell me," I ordered, forcing Anya's shift.

"He sent us away." She squeezed her eyes shut and turned over to face the sparkling water.

"Explain." It wasn't necessary to say please. I was Panteris and she knew it. Frankly, I'd been there and experienced a mate's refusal.

She stiffened and glared at me. "I have no idea what you want me to say. He fucked me and asked for my bite, and then he rejected me." She crouched over bent knees. "I want to go back to Earth."

"Males are stupid. Rakon did the same thing to me. Go back to Denkar tomorrow."

Anya peered up at me. "He won't accept me."

"Did you give him your mating bite?" She nodded and lowered her head.

Ximeran males were idiots. "Yeah. Go back tomorrow. Rakon ended up in confinement for it."

She propped herself up on her elbow, her bare breasts pressed into the sand. "Really?"

"The First Councilor called him an idiot and made him stay there all night. I watched vids with his science officer and ate popcorn."

Anya flopped to her back and sighed. "Tomorrow. It's nice here and I don't have anywhere else to go."

I didn't say anything, but I didn't think Denkar would make her wait that long. "You can stay here tonight if you like. In the meantime, I have something to keep us busy."

She hopped to her feet and lowered her head. "My apologies, Panteris. I should have made an appointment, but I'll try to stay out of your way."

I chuckled. "Actually, I'm glad you're here. I could use a hand cleaning the house. It's been in Rakon's family for a long time, and they've used it for storage. It looks like... I don't know what, but it's full of old furniture and trash."

Her eyes brightened and she cracked a smile. "I'd be happy to assist. Maybe we can save some things to help the other shifters set up their homes when they arrive."

"That's a wonderful idea!" I took her hand and we walked back to the house. The meal had improved my attitude and Anya's generous offer of help was very welcome. It would take a lot less time with two of us.

We dressed and detoured to the kitchen for water to wash down the delicious fish and got started. It was nice to work with another shifter. I hadn't realized how much I'd missed the company of another creature who understood my nature.

We collapsed into a rather wonderful couch and shared a bottle of wine she'd found in an old box. Neither of us would get drunk, of course, but the pale, effervescent fluid was refreshing and sweet. I brushed the dust off the label and blinked at the words.

"I think it's French."

"Really? I can read a little bit." She held out her hand and I passed the bottle to her. She wiped at it with the tail of her shirt and squinted. "It says Dom Per... Something. It's too faded to read."

"I wonder who brought it to Ximera."

"Panterum might know. There are several more bottles in that box over there."

I nodded and took another drink from the aged bottle as I looked at the results of our labors. The room still bore a thick coating of dust and boxes littered the space, but we'd gotten most of it sorted. Sadly, the pile of trash was much larger than the neat collection of things I wanted to keep.

Neither of us could figure out what to do with the trash, but it was probably a good idea to let Rakon have a chance at it. I didn't recognize many of the things, but he probably would.

When we'd finished the wine, I asked, "Do you want to go for a swim?"

"Is it safe?"

I had to think about it for a moment. Rakon hadn't said there was any danger, and the guards that had dogged my steps in the Council building had been assigned to other duties. "I think so. Rakon didn't mention any danger and there aren't any people around." I lifted my shoulders into a shrug. "Besides, we've already gone fishing and nothing happened."

She grinned and stripped out of her clothes. "Race you!"

I laughed and dropped my dress to the floor, shifting into my tiger as I chased her. She was a better swimmer, but I was faster and caught up easily. It was so wonderful to have a friend again.

RAKON

I hated having to cool my heels waiting for the first councilor to show up. Hadn't he requested this meeting? Unfortunately, no one could tell me his location and I wondered if he'd forgotten me.

It hadn't been a completely wasted trip, though. I managed to set up several teams to return to Earth for the wolves and orca shifters located in Alaska, plus another group to search the southern coastline of the mainland near where Renata had lived.

And I'd managed to make contact with Markon. He spared a brief moment to snarl at me that he was closing in on the pirate that had been plaguing the outer sectors.

I wished him all the best with that endeavor.

I ordered lunch while I waited for the First, but I'd run out of patience by the time I'd finished eating. I wanted to get home to Renata. As I was leaving a message with his assistant, he strode in, his robes flying behind him.

Scowling at me, he asked, "What are you doing here? Shouldn't you be with that pretty tiger of yours?"

"You summoned me here for a meeting." I looked at my comm, and added, "Almost two hours ago."

"I did no such thing. You're off duty until you convince Renata to come to her senses and take her place on my Council."

"I received a message just this morning from you. You said you wanted to discuss missions to retrieve the Earth shifters. I've done as you asked and prepped several crews for the recovery efforts."

He sobered and his eyes turned hard. "No, Commander. I sent no such message." He spun to face his assistant. "Is there a note in my personal calendar?"

"No, sir. I assumed you'd made arrangements with the commander verbally, and I had just come in when he arrived."

"Get my personal guard loaded and on their way to…"

I didn't hear the rest. I was already out the door. Someone had set me up and I'd left Renata alone and vulnerable. How could I have been so stupid?

The propulsion unit on my personal transport whined as I took the craft into the lower atmosphere. I hadn't done such tricks since I was a boy, but I wasn't interested in dealing with the heavy traffic surrounding the capital city. I sent my prayers to all the ancient gods and hoped I'd reach her in time.

~

RENATA

We chuffed happily as the bear bowled us over into the sand and chewed on our neck. Our paws scrabbled at her belly fur, claws sheathed so we didn't hurt her. I couldn't remember the last time we'd played. We frolicked like cubs, rolling in the surf as we mock battled for dominance.

We gnawed on her foreleg and she yelped but allowed us to soothe the hurt with our rough tongue as she did the same to our neck fur. We curled up together in the shade, exhausted from our play.

Despite missing our mate, we'd had a wonderful day with our Kodiak friend.

We heard the sudden noise of a transport and lifted our head. Had Rakon returned? Squinting, we searched out the sound and found a small interstellar craft hovering several meters away. It wasn't Rakon's.

We stood and peered at the craft. Had Denkar already come to retrieve Anya? The males that exited the craft weren't anyone we recognized. They had positioned themselves downwind of us and left no scent we could discern.

One of the males lifted something to a shoulder and we heard a soft pop as Anya roared in pain and tried to get to her feet. She whimpered as she took a step forward and collapsed to the wet sand.

We growled low in our throat as one of the males lifted the thing that had hurt Anya once more, dodging to the side when we heard the pop of sound. We hated that she'd gotten hit with another projectile, but used her still form for cover. It would do neither of us any good if we couldn't fight.

From behind us, two more of those pops were loud in our ears and our haunch went numb as blackness covered our vision. We heard male laughter as rough hands loaded us into the transport. We tried to cover Anya, but they tore us away from her as the transport accelerated into the atmosphere.

RAKON

I raced toward the hovering transport, desperate to reach it before they loaded my mate and Anya. They were both too still and I watched in horror as the unidentified crew loaded them on a hover board.

I felt the sting as their blaster shots burned my skin, but I didn't stop until they lifted from the ground. One of the First's guards lifted his weapon and fired at the departing transport, but I slapped him down.

"My mate is on that transport, jackass! Get a tracker on it. I want to know everything you can find out about it. Find the owner and anything you can on the crew."

He cowered away at my angry growl, but he wasn't my target. I wanted whoever had ordered this attack, and my best hope would be working through his own first shift about now. If Anya was with Renata, he'd pushed her away as I'd done to my own mate. I raced back to my transport and prayed Anya hadn't given him her bite. That wasn't likely though, so I prayed he'd be lucid enough to hunt.

Two hours later, I found him gorging on the carcass of a *dikar*. The animal had been stripped of flesh and he chewed on the remnants of a long bone, licking away the marrow from the cracked femur.

"Get up!"

Denkar's bear snarled at me, and I knew he'd lost himself to the creature inside him. I didn't have time to let him come back to himself on his own. I needed his help. I tried to remember how Renata had exerted her power over Anya. She was a born Panteris and it might be natural to her, but I had to try.

We are Panterum. Let me.

I stepped back and allowed the tiger to take control. The rush of energy nearly dropped me to my knees, but I held steady. "Shift, Denkar. Our mates have been taken."

The bear roared as he shifted, a mixture of pain and rage in his voice. "Kill you," he growled as he leaped toward me.

I held up a hand, my body thrumming with barely contained energy. "Do not fuck with me, Kodiak."

Denkar fell to his knees, his breaths heaving. "Forgive me, Panterum. I..."

"Forget it. Pull yourself together. I need a tracker."

He stood and nodded, but his muscles trembled as he tried to shake off the bear's control and stop himself from shifting. "They took my Anya and the War Mate?"

"Yes. Unmarked Mendaran transport. I have a trace put on it so I hope we can follow it."

"It will head for one of the outposts. They have to know that seventeen is watched too closely."

"Yes, and that's where you come in."

He grinned and I saw teeth behind the smile. "Ready to learn to be a smuggler, Commander?"

I returned the smile as the emerging stripes warmed my face. "It's about damned time."

CHAPTER
FOURTEEN

RENATA

I don't know how long we were unconscious, but the sound of soft weeping made me try to lift my head to see who cried. I stiffened in horror at my surroundings.

Cages. Dozens of them of varying sizes, about half of which were filled with young shifters barely out of spiky cub fur, but all in their human shapes. There were a couple of males, but the vast majority were female. A few might have been old enough to deliver a mating bite, but I doubted it.

I couldn't help my angry growl when I saw they all wore collars. Was this some sort of sick zoo? My head swam as I tried to get to my feet and shift so I could speak to the terrified cubs staring at me. A low buzz tickled my neck and I realized I wore one of those blasted collars as well.

I couldn't reach for the change. The tiger was there; I felt her. But it was like trying to reach through a steel wall. I huffed out a breath and sat on my haunches as I considered my predicament and tried to figure out how to free the captive cubs.

Anya snorted on the floor next to me. She'd gotten a double dose of whatever drug they'd used to immobilize us. I hoped it hadn't harmed her, but hearing her raspy breaths made me hope she'd wake up soon.

I wanted to start taking pieces off whoever had found a drug that would knock a shifter sideways.

I wished I could speak to the cubs. Where had they come from? I knew there were at least two jackals; the dusty, dry scent of them was unmistakable and I was familiar with it from my time with Sendra. I had no idea what the rest of them were. A half-remembered meeting with a wolf was the only time I'd ever come into contact with another shifter. I didn't trust my memory, but I also didn't believe there were wolves in this sad collection.

The door slammed open and I watched the cubs huddle into the backs of their cages. Turning, I faced the new threat, determined to protect them. I smelled him before I saw him, the reeking scent of hate and unwashed male preceding him.

Norkad. That fucking asshole. My lips pulled back from my fangs and I snarled. I watched with more than a little satisfaction as he limped into the room, leaning heavily on a crutch. He smirked at me and touched a button on the comm in his hand.

The collar around my neck vibrated once and grew hot. I didn't have time to take a breath before it sent a bolt of electricity through my body, dropping me to the floor. It hurt just as badly as that damned shock stick, but worse because it didn't stop. It was in contact with my flesh.

My bladder released and I heard him laugh. "All right, War Mate. Shift now and the collar will stop hurting you."

I ignored him and tried to breathe through the pain, but the current increased until I yowled in agony. The tiger sprang forward, pushing me into my human form despite my angry refusal. While I knew we would not be his pet or his whore or anything else, she only wanted the pain to stop.

We were helpless when he kicked Anya awake and subjected her to the same torture, leaving her sobbing quietly on the floor.

I curled up into a ball, panting heavily as Norkad chuckled and thumbed another button. The current stopped and I tried to hold back my relieved sigh. The collar sent a pulse into my skin and I twitched as the steel wall blocked me from my tiger once more.

"Handy little gadget, don't you think?"

He used the tip of his crutch to tap the collar around my throat and I wanted to take it away from him and shove it up his ass. The reminder of the painful shock was the only thing keeping me still.

I didn't answer and he scowled. "Enjoy the rest of your life, bitch. I'll think about you when I spend the money you and your mutant friends earn me." After one last prod to my ribs, he limped out, slamming the door behind him. The metallic clicks of a lock were loud in the quiet space.

"I can't believe we let a one-legged humanoid best us." Anya growled. "Have we gotten so weak?"

"He had two legs at our last meeting. I gave it to Rakon as a mating gift."

She blinked at me and chuckled. "I shall give Denkar the other. Will it please him?"

"I think they should share his head."

Nodding solemnly, she said, "That would be appropriate."

I groaned as I hauled myself to my feet and tottered over to a cot against the far wall. There were pants and a couple of shirts, but no underwear or shoes. The clothes were made of thin gray fabric with orange crosses decorating the backs. Prison uniforms, perhaps? I didn't care about nudity, but I didn't want to wander around bare-assed in front of cubs any longer than I had to. Anya grabbed a shirt and pants for herself and we dressed silently.

"What should we do, Panteris?"

"We're getting the cubs out of those stupid cages."

She grunted and started breaking locks with her strong fingers.

They'd been meant to contain young shifters and were no match for an adult Kodiak. I started on the other side, leaving the doors open as I went, but none of the cubs would come out.

I wasn't sure why I was surprised. They'd been conditioned to think of those cages as their dens and were faced with two unknown adult shifters. I didn't have any food to entice them. Anya touched my arm and tilted her head toward the cot.

I nodded and we settled ourselves on the thin mattress. The bed creaked alarmingly under our weight but held as we waited to see if there was a brave one in that crowd of terrified cubs. We talked softly of our mates and of the verdant green that was Ximera 8, knowing they heard our words.

Our patience was soon rewarded when a very thin young boy crept warily from his cage, pulling along a slightly older girl. The resemblance was striking and I knew they must be siblings. Despite the clear signs of neglect on their scrawny bodies, the cubs were beautiful and I wondered what they were. Their hair was long, but tightly curled and spread out in wiry halos around their heads. Black eyes glittered like gemstones in mahogany skin.

I wanted to gather them both into my lap and hug them but forced myself to be still and let them approach in their own time. The boy drew himself up and held out his free hand.

"I am Muhammad and this is my sister, Lotus. We are leopards. Have you come to rescue us?"

"I am Renata, a tiger, and I will do my best. Do you know where we are?"

"It is a place called sector four, but I do not remember a country on Earth by that name."

Dangerous alien fauna. "We're not on Earth. We're in the Ximeran system."

He nodded sadly. "I didn't think so. Will we be able to go home?"

"If I can get us free, you may either return to Earth or come with me to Ximera 8. Do you have family on Earth?"

"My father is leader of our clan." His thin shoulders drew straight and he stared at me proudly.

I had to hold in a chuckle. He was so darned cute and the nascent power wafting from him told me he'd be a wonderful Pardus in his own time. "That's good news. As I said, you may return if you wish. You may also ask your clan if they would like to emigrate to Ximera."

"You overstep, tiger. Leopards have better sense than to stay in a place where we will be caged."

"Respect, cub. You speak to the Panteris." Anya's low growl of annoyance made the cubs back away and I put a hand on her arm.

"It's okay. And he's right. Neither of us left Earth willingly, remember?"

"True."

Muhammad gave her a distrustful look and led his sister back to their cages. I sighed unhappily. The cubs had no reason to trust me, and I refused to use my influence as Panteris to force them to bend to me. I just hoped we could get them back to their families.

The lights flashed, hurting my eyes just as the door opened. Three men entered, two carrying large sacks, while the third carried a shock stick. Without speaking or acknowledging our presence, they upended the sacks, allowing raw meat to fall to the floor.

I curled my lip. It was replicated, but would meet the cubs' nutritional needs. Muhammad and his sister glared at us as if daring us to take the food. My heart broke as he carefully divided it into portions, his sister delivering it to the cages. When they'd finished, he grudgingly brought a share to Anya and me.

"We share here. This is yours."

"Give it to the smallest ones," Anya muttered. "We've already eaten." She waited until he reached his cage and whispered, "They keep cubs hungry. I shall feed their keepers to them in recompense."

"Hold that thought." I didn't need to add that we'd have to get free of these damned collars first.

The lights went out, leaving us in darkness. I heard a few of the cubs whimper, but movement told me that they were giving comfort to each other now that they were free to leave their cages. Settling back against Anya, I closed my eyes and tried to rest.

RAKON

I slammed my fist down on the arm of my chair. "How the fuck did we lose them so fast?"

Denkar typed furiously at his panel and ignored me. His bear was focused on his task and hadn't eaten more than a mouthful or two of replicated meat and only when Medic Krenak threatened to have him medically confined.

Three fucking days and we hadn't seen a single trace of the unidentified transport that had stolen our mates. There were four of that type known to be in Ximeran space. One had been reported stolen, and two were accounted for in dock for repairs.

Interestingly enough, Markon reported the stolen transport was currently in his pirate's possession, but he was unable to locate them. I shook my head at the thought of Markon. He smiled in every communication and the first councilor had demanded to know why he was laughing and polite.

I had to wonder if the chase had made him descend into the madness that had dogged him for so many years.

"Got the slimy little fucker!"

Denkar's shout made me flinch and stripes warmed my face. "Excuse me?"

"I never bothered to look there because it's in the middle of our own space and barely a day from Ximera 8. The energy trail from that ship goes directly to sector four." He tapped a few more keys on his panel. "And there's record of them landing at the space dock near the containment facility."

"That's restricted space. Why would they have gone there?"

"Your guess is as good as mine, but I suggest you get the First on the comm and get permission to land."

I typed the message and sent it off. The First Councilor would arrange clearance for us to land. I doubted we'd find our mates there, but it was the only lead we had. I gave the order and we turned toward sector four.

Denkar rubbed his face, his exhaustion clear. "I'm going to sleep for a few hours. Wake me when we reach orbit."

I decided he'd had a good idea and returned to my quarters for some much-needed rest and a shower. I allowed myself an hour and spent the rest of my time watching old Earth vids. Despite my exhaustion, I wasn't going to get any sleep.

The chime of a comm from the first councilor interrupted *Leave it to Beaver* and I switched the vidscreen over to receive his message. His angry countenance filled my screen.

"The containment facility on sector four has refused permission to land, despite my order to the contrary. They say they've had a breach and a biological contaminant has escaped."

I stood up, hope filling me. They were trying to hide something, and I suspected that something had black-and-white stripes. "What are your orders, sir?"

"I'm sending Markon and Dakar to meet you. It will take them some time, but you should expect them in less than twelve hours. When they get there, I want you three to remind those white-coated freaks who runs this system."

He narrowed his eyes, bushy brows drawing together in an ugly scowl. "Bring whoever you find back to Ximera 8 to face charges. I can't make an example of your mate refusing my orders because she'll eat me, but I'll be damned if some ill-mannered medic with an ego is going to get the better of me."

"Yes, sir." I grinned as Fengar cut the communication short. I really had to talk to Renata about taking her place on the Council. Fengar wasn't having a very good cycle.

Dakar scowled at me when I passed along Fengar's order but agreed to change course to meet us. He had a lead on Daiyu and wasn't happy to have to leave it. Markon was already on his way, chasing his pirate, but he didn't know why they'd head toward sector four.

I laughed as I strode toward Denkar's quarters. These cats were running us in circles. I couldn't blame them, though. I knew Renata wanted nothing more than to nest and make cubs. Given her choice, I had a feeling she'd never set foot in another transport.

～

RENATA

Emergency lights flashed and I heard shouts from the corridor outside our cell as the building shuddered around us. Anya and I leaped to our feet, trying to locate the cubs in the dim illumination.

"It's an earthquake, I think. We used to get them in Alaska sometimes."

A concussive explosion threw us both to the floor amid the screams of the terrified cubs. Rubble fell from the ceiling, and I crawled over to reach her.

"Earthquake, huh?"

She grinned, the blood from a nasty cut on her face seeping down to stain the gray prison uniform. "Prison break?"

"We can only hope." I stood up and glared at the cages. "Come on out, everyone! I think we have a chance to escape!"

None of the cubs moved, their wide eyes glinting at me as they huddled deeper into their tiny sanctuaries. I hadn't wanted to force them, but I couldn't risk them being hurt.

Power filled me and I shrieked when the collar around my neck sparked out and fell open. It left a nasty burn on the side of my neck, but it was worth another scar to be free of the damned thing. I wished I had the time and the nerve to try removing the disgusting things from the cubs.

"All of you, get out here right now!" I didn't shout. There wasn't a need for any Panteris to speak above a whisper. When the last cub cowered at my feet, I relented.

"I'm so sorry I had to scare you, but you must listen to me and follow as close as you—"

The cubs screamed in fear as the door exploded inward. I used my body to cover as many as I could as a short woman dressed in black strode into the cell.

"Rescue, party of..." She pulled a helmet from her head, exposing long black hair and a face spotted with rosettes. "A few more than I expected. It's good to meet you, Panteris."

"Soledad." I nodded my head in acknowledgment. Even if I hadn't seen a photo of her, I recognized the scent of cat. This jaguar deserved my respect. "Everyone is looking for you."

Her full lips twitched into a smile. "Looking isn't finding. You may tell Commander Markon that I'll eat him if he keeps bothering me. He'll be delicious with hot sauce."

Another explosion made me flinch away. That one had been too close. Soledad scowled and glanced out the door as she tossed me a comm.

"I'm afraid I don't have time to chat. Your knights errant have come to save the day and that little slime Norkad has already left." She grinned at me, showing teeth. "And congratulations for taking a bite out of him, Panteris. I'll deliver the rest of him when I catch up to the skinny fucker. Alive, of course. My mating gift to you will be dinner and a show."

She laughed at her joke and pointed at the comm in my hand. "If you decide to renounce your utterly boring lives of matehood and domesticity, the comm contains the control access to a sweet little ride parked at the space dock. I'm afraid you'll have to find me your-selves if you want to join my merry band."

Without another word, she vanished into the smoke-filled corridor, leaving us staring after her. "Well... That was interesting," I murmured. I had no idea what to say. Soledad looked healthy, if not completely happy. We sensed so much rage from her it occurred to me to try to force her to wait until her mate caught her.

Yet she'd escaped too quickly, as if she expected me to order her compliance as Panteris. I wasn't interested in taking her free will. If her mate wanted her that badly, they'd have to work it out themselves.

Anya and I herded the cubs into a tight group and led them through the dusty corridor. The raised voices were easy to follow, and we soon found our mates arguing with a medic in a white coat as Rakon's crewmates secured him with restraints.

Denkar saw Anya first and raced toward her, swinging her into his arms with a happy cry as he kissed her. The look on Rakon's face when he saw me made my knees weak, but I ignored the shaking in my limbs and met him halfway. I leaped into his embrace, wrapping my legs around his hips.

He buried his face in my hair. "Don't ever do that again, mate. We thought we'd lost you." His hands clenched my waist hard enough I would probably have bruises, but I didn't care.

I knew my days of relative freedom without the presence of guards was at an end. I didn't care about that either. If we'd had guards... I refused to continue the thought. It didn't matter because it had given me the opportunity to rescue the cubs.

Angry shouts and squeals of fear pulled my attention toward the group of cubs, and I struggled away from Rakon's arms as his crew surrounded them. A tall, furious male held Muhammad off the ground with a bleeding hand as the cub snapped and hissed at him.

"Put him down!" I roared. I used every ounce of authority I could muster and watched in satisfaction as the cub's bare feet hit the floor.

"The little shit bit me!"

"You probably deserved it." I tugged Muhammad behind me and faced the angry Ximeran. "The cubs are terrified and hungry, and you grabbed him? Are you crazy?"

Rakon's strong arms wrapped around me, pulling me back and keeping me from setting my teeth in the arrogant male. "Renata, I'd like to present my old friend, Markon."

I cocked my head to the, then burst into laughter. "I have a message for you, Commander Markon. Your mate says that if you keep bothering her, she's going to eat you with hot sauce."

"I beg your pardon?"

"Soledad says she's too busy for you, and that you should leave her alone."

He reached forward to grab me, but I bared my fangs and snapped. He held up his hands and jumped back. "She was here?"

"She helped us get out and left her transport. I assume she had another ride waiting."

His hands clenched, and he breathed hard through his nose. I knew that if he hadn't been worried about losing a hand, he'd have tried to shake me. "I swear to the ancient gods that woman won't sit down for a week when I get hold of her." He turned away without waiting for an answer and left the room.

"Good luck with that," I muttered.

"How badly is she likely to hurt him?" Rakon asked.

"No idea, but I think I'd like to watch."

RAKON

It took forever to load the staff from the containment facility. There were dozens; too many to have all been in on the unlawful confinement of the children. We still had to figure out who was involved, so they all had to go.

The children were another matter entirely. The oldest, a handsome youth with dark skin, was adamant they be returned to Earth and refused to board my battle cruiser until Renata spoke with him. Her power flooded the room and I knew she compelled him.

I didn't want to return any of the children to the dubious comfort and safety of Earth, but it was their choice. And it wasn't safe for them to remain in sector four. Renata clearly hated the idea too.

We eventually got everyone safely back to Ximera 8 and put the scientists into containment cells. They could be someone else's problem. I wanted to take my mate home.

Denkar and Anya had slipped out, escaping the confusion and barked orders. I envied them their freedom.

"By the stars..." The First's whispered prayer came from behind me, and I turned to look at him. He had tears glinting in his eyes as he looked at the children huddled in a corner. "They're... babies. Little ones."

He pushed past me and limped toward the children, leaning heavily on his cane. They stared at him, expressions of shock on their little faces as he settled himself on a bench in their midst. A small girl with huge brown eyes approached him, clambering on his lap to tug his beard. He let out a choked laugh and pulled her gently into his arms, resting his face against her blonde hair.

"Why does the old one cry?"

I hadn't seen the dark-skinned boy sidle up beside me. He was clearly their leader, and his burgeoning power was evident to my tiger. "We haven't seen children in many years. You are... precious to us."

He snorted, his disbelief evident. "Precious enough to cage us."

"No. Precious enough that the entire population will die to protect you."

He ignored me and stared at the First. Other children cuddled close, and I knew they were desperate for the physical contact with someone who wouldn't hurt them. "Very well. I will examine your Ximera and decide for myself whether it is suitable for my clan. You will escort me."

I wanted to laugh at his imperious tone, but Renata poked me in the ribs as he continued speaking.

"You are highly ranked, and it is only fitting."

"I will do as you ask in exchange for information." The boy's eyebrow rose in interest, and I wanted to grin. "I want the location of your clan and any other shifter group that you know."

"Why would I give you that knowledge?"

"You will give it to me because I have the means to protect them. Your enemies already know the location, and I want them to rest easy on Earth whether they choose to emigrate or not."

He nodded, his expression sad and solemn. "You will find the leopards in Kenya, along with a small group of cheetahs. The lions and hyenas left before the storms but there are jackals in Morocco."

"Thank you, Muhammad," Renata said, her voice soft. "You may come with us or stay with the other children with the first councilor. He will care for you and make sure you have enough to eat."

He glanced over at the children, narrowing his eyes as his sister crawled into the First's lap. "I will stay. You may return tomorrow for my tour."

I took Renata's hand and led her away. Fengar was too busy with the children to pay us any heed, and we took shameless advantage of his inattention. I helped her into my vehicle, kissing her thoroughly as I strapped her in.

"What was that for?" A small smile played about her lips, and I kissed her again.

"Because I can. I hope you're well-rested because I plan to do many other things to you before we sleep."

I settled myself next to her and her eyes dilated with arousal. I almost wished we had a driver so I could address her needs, but we'd be home soon enough. I loved that word home.

With luck, we'd have peace, but that wasn't likely. We still needed to locate Chen Daiyu, along with Soledad Martinez and her sisters, and I had a feeling neither of them would come to their new home without a fight.

Still, despite our lingering worries, I had my mate. That was enough for now.

~

IF YOU'RE LOOKING for more of Minette's stories featuring creatures that go bump in the night, check out Wicked Truth wherever e-books are sold.

ACKNOWLEDGMENTS

As always, my undying gratitude goes out to Engineer Hubby, Mr. Greywood-Moreau, for his love, encouragement, and support. Without him, I don't think I'd be writing at all. Love you to the moon and back, baby.

Want to see what I'm up to next? Join Raisa's Renegades. You can also sign up for my newsletter to get a free Wicked Magic story delivered straight to your inbox!

About Minette Moreau

Minette is the alter-ego of USA Today bestselling author Raisa Greywood, and writes all the things that go bump in the night. Shapeshifters, aliens, vampires, and especially dragons all find their way into her stories.

www.minettemoreau.com

[f] facebook.com/AuthorMinetteMoreau
[BB] bookbub.com/authors/minette-moreau
[g] goodreads.com/minettemoreau

Also by Minette Moreau

Shifters' Mates

Tiger's Gambit

Leopard's Surrender

Jaguar's Initiative

Wicked Magic

Wicked Truth

Wicked Fire

Wicked Rage

www.ingramcontent.com/pod-product-compliance
Lightning Source LLC
Chambersburg PA
CBHW030314180626
46810CB00003B/1073